THE ZIGZAG WAY

ANITA DESAI

THE ZIGZAG WAY

Chatto & Windus

LONDON

Published by Chatto & Windus 2004

2 4 6 8 10 9 7 5 3 1

Copyright © Anita Desai 2004

First published in Great Britain in 2004 by
Chatto & Windus
Random House, 20 Vauxhall Bridge Road,
London SW1V 2SA

Random House Australia (Pty) Limited
20 Alfred Street, Milsons Point, Sydney
New South Wales 2061, Australia

Random House New Zealand Limited
18 Poland Road, Glenfield,
Auckland 10, New Zealand

Random House (Pty) Limited
Endulini, 5A Jubilee Road, Parktown 2193, South Africa

The Random House Group Limited Reg. No. 954009
www.randomhouse.co.uk

A CIP catalogue record for this book
is available from the British Library

ISBN 0 7011 7743 8

Typeset in Janson by Palimpsest Book Production Limited,
Polmont, Stirlingshire

Printed and bound in Great Britain by
Mackays of Chatham plc, Chatham, Kent

TO KIRAN, WITH THANKS
FOR HER COMPANIONSHIP

After half an hour's silence my brother irrelevantly exclaimed:

'What agreeable people one runs across in queer, out-of-the-way places!'

'Who on earth are you thinking of now?' I enquired.

'Why, I was thinking of *us*!' he placidly replied, and went on with his reading.

Charles Macomb Flandreu, Viva Mexico!, 1908

PART I

Eric Arrives

The ancient Chinese believed time is not a ladder one ascends into the future but a ladder one descends into the past.

Chapter 1

                                    . . . Oh, tourist,
    is this how this country is going to answer you

    and your immodest demands for a different world,
    and a better life, and complete comprehension
    of both at last, and immediately . . .
                Elizabeth Bishop, 'Arrival at Santos', 1952

'There is only the one inn,' he was told when, on getting off the bus, he asked where he might stay.

Since the inn was directly across the square from where the bus had stopped, he could not have missed it even in the dusk. The wind that had scraped and scoured the hills around till the stones gleamed white now struck the tin signboard against the wall of the inn with the sound of a bell striking the hours, drawing his attention to it.

He buttoned up his jacket, sank his chin into the folds of his scarf, picked up his bag and set off towards the house on a path under the casuarina trees, passing an empty fountain with a broken spout. The houses around the square were all shut and dark, no window or door to let light fall across the pillared arcades except for the store at the corner where a few men had gathered under a bare electric bulb as if for warmth; it was from them he had enquired about lodgings. Now they watched him as he crossed the square to the inn and continued to watch as he knocked again and again at the door. If they said anything to each other, he could not hear them for the sound of the wind coming through the casuarinas and the tin signboard beating.

Finally, a woman let him in. She was engaged in conversation with someone in the room behind and did not stay but withdrew, leaving him in the darkness of the hall. He could make out a desk, a massive carved one like a house with many doors, all shut, but no one attended it. A row of keys hung from a shelf above it on which some short stout candles flickered and poured out pools of soft tallow. They cast their uncertain light on a skull with green sequins for eyes and a circlet of gilt marigolds for a crown. Above this, on the wall, whole skeletons danced and cavorted, rustling in the draught from the door, for they were cut out of paper.

He watched them and listened to a clock ticking somewhere, mesmerised. In the room beyond he could see light and a fire, people and movement – real, living, not papery or skeletal or funereal. The clattering sound of metal pans and earthenware told him it was the kitchen. That was promising, but no one seemed interested in the appearance of a stranger.

Eventually someone, someone else, did come down a staircase from the upper regions of the house and greeted him, a young woman with her dark hair tied back in a ribbon. She pushed up the sleeves of her red sweater as if for business and when he asked if she had a room, slid a form across the desk for him to fill in. 'How many nights?' she asked, but when she saw him hesitate,

4

shrugged, indicating he could put down what he liked, it did not matter. Unhooking an iron key eight or ten inches long, she offered to show him a room.

He followed her down a dark stairwell which had dim lamps attached to a stone wall at such long intervals that there were stretches of stone steps where no light was cast at all. Deeper and deeper down she took him, her felt slippers making no sound, and it was as if they were going further and further back in time, finally reaching a period that was surely medieval, for the door they arrived at seemed hewn with an axe; when she turned the immense key in its immense lock, it creaked open on what he feared would be a cellar if not a dungeon.

Instead, when she switched on an electric light, the room blazed into colour, proving improbably cheerful. There was a vast bed heaped with red cushions on a white counterpane, a sheepskin rug on the floor and white cotton curtains at a high, small window. She spun the tap at the washbasin to show him it worked and water flowed, and smiled to see him smile with relief, lower his bag on to a chair and nod to indicate he would take the room.

'Upstairs is the restaurant where you may eat,' she told him and, laying out a clean towel for him, disappeared.

As he washed his face with a block of soap, then scrubbed with the thick, dry towel, he thought of the days and nights he had spent on the train, slowly, sadly rattling over the lonely plains, struggling to achieve the horizon where hills rose to break the oppressive flatness only to find them mysteriously receding and remaining elusive, and then the hours on the bus through the valley with its strange twisted forms of cacti rising out of the volcanic

5

rubble like stakes rising from secret graves. He had almost ceased to believe the town existed, that it was anything more than a legend, this ghost town of the sierra.

This perception had been magnified on entering the inn; now he felt slightly ashamed of his lack of faith, the many weak moments of panic he had had. He thought of himself cutting the figure of a timid pilgrim who sinks down in despair again and again along the way, needing to be coaxed and assisted into rising and going on, and avoided looking at himself in the tin-framed mirror as he rubbed his hair dry.

Upstairs, in the restaurant, the door to the kitchen stood open. Light streamed in as well as the sounds of pots rattling and voices animated by food, drink and company. The aroma of food being prepared over open fires was enough to raise his wavering spirits and make him anticipate the comfort of a meal and a drink. Some of the tables were already occupied. Two men who looked like officials sat drinking beer and eating nachos, expansive in their gestures and speech as if pleased with themselves and how profitably their day had passed. At another table, some young men, still boys, alternately brushed back their hair and drank from bottles of Coca-Cola, then got up to go into the kitchen and returned with plates of food. In a corner, an elderly couple sat trying to feed a small boy who knelt on the bench beside them but seemed more interested in playing with his bowl of soup than in eating from it. They coaxed him; he turned his head away and splashed the soup with his spoon.

Then a young man came out of the kitchen where he had been laughing so that the after-image of his laugh

6

lingered on his face, and crossed the room to their table, took the spoon away and sat down, taking the child on his lap and indicating that he would feed him.

It was a domestic scene and Eric was not particularly drawn to domesticity but, deciding there was enough evidence of nourishment, chose a nearby table and waited for a menu to be presented. One of the women in the kitchen came out and handed him one and he ordered a bottle of red wine straight away, with food to follow. As he expected, most of the items on the menu proved unavailable – they had, in fact, seemed a bit improbable – only one dish was actually available and it was brought to him, undeniably hot and reviving. He drank, ate and watched the family at the neighbouring table more tolerantly: domesticity clearly had its points.

But now the child slipped off the young man's lap and ran about the room, shouting in triumph at his escape. The elders all laughed. The child had the transparent grey-blue eyes and head of silky golden curls that make anyone popular at first glance. The young man possessed a slightly more worn version. The older couple was short and dark which made the child's fairness the more distinctive.

Suddenly, unexpectedly, he darted across to Eric's table and began to bang his spoon on its edge as if aware he was both naughty and pretty and would attract attention but not censure. The young man, the father, came rushing over to pick him up in his arms and kiss him, laughing. Then he apologised to Eric and sat down at his table, holding the child on his lap.

'He has only just learned to run – and so he runs everywhere. He makes us run too,' he explained. 'If we don't catch him, he will run out on the street, he is so quick.'

7

'It seems safe,' Eric replied. 'There is no traffic.'

'Oh, it is coming, coming soon, more every day – for the festival, you know,' the young man said. 'Many come for the *Día de los Muertos* here. It is – it is –' he rolled his eyes and held a hand in the air to indicate its importance.

He had an accent Eric could not place precisely: it might have been German, Austrian – perhaps Swiss? As if aware of this speculation, the young man held out his hand and introduced himself. 'André Bernstein,' he announced, and of course that could be from any one those countries, thought Eric.

'Have you been here long?' he asked, not being able to think of a more original opening to a dialogue in a Mexican inn in a town visited by tourists.

'Here? Four years now. I came to spend one night in the inn, met Paola, never left,' he laughed, happily. 'She cast a spell – like in a fairy story, no?'

Eric thought that if it were like a spell in a fairy story, then it was bound to break one day which would be sad for the father who was playing so delightedly with his son, capturing him every time he tried to slip away. Eventually the child did wriggle free and escape, choosing the moment when the father launched upon his story, one he clearly enjoyed telling. It was a fairly common-place story for these times – about a boy who had grown up in a small town in the Alps, developed the 'wander-lust' he said, made his way on a cargo ship to Costa Rica, then gone backpacking north into Guatemala and to Yucatán where he ran into the rainy season and with it the swarms of mosquitoes that found his blood sweet to devour, came down with malaria and began to pine for mountain air. Northwards, then, to the high sierra where

8

he recovered his health – and, in Paola, so much more. His expression melted like butter, in uxurious bliss.

'Other foreigners have come here and stayed too, have they not?' Eric probed, his tiredness combining with the red wine to make him less nimble, less discreet than he was by nature.

He saw at once that he had been clumsy and too abrupt by the way the fair-haired man's expression altered as if the soft butter, the melting wax of it, had suddenly stiffened. He no longer looked so pleased as when he was telling his 'fairy story'. Eric was clearly suggesting that it was not an uncommon story, that it was much the same as that of others – and no one cares to hear that. Each stranger, each traveller needs to think his story unique.

But having blundered, Eric felt helpless to stop himself. 'Doña Vera who lives in the Hacienda de la Soledad below, that is her story too, perhaps?'

Now the young man looked at him, astounded. Then he bent over with laughter. He tipped back his chair and roared with it, his face flushed with it. As he laughed and continued to laugh, Eric found himself flushing too, with annoyance. He failed to see the joke and was about to say so when André spluttered, 'So, you are one of *those*, eh?'

'One of – ?'

'Those who travel to her hacienda – de la Soledad, ha! – to pay homage –' he began to chuckle again, helplessly – 'homage to *la Reina de la Sierra*. Is that not how she is known to all of you?'

'I had never even heard of her a week ago,' Eric protested, 'and did not come for her sake but for the mountain –'

'Oh. Ah. The magic mushroom then, the peyote?'

'No,' Eric protested with force, and was wondering if it would be a good idea to confide in this light-hearted listener what had really brought him here, when it became evident that the listener had lost interest, or become distracted, having suddenly remembered his son and noted his absence.

'Sebastian,' he cried in alarm, looking about him wildly, 'where are you?' and he darted out of a door that opened not into the square that Eric had come through but on to a narrow side street.

Of course that was just when the child's mother appeared – the woman with the dark hair in a red ribbon who had let him in. Looking around, she too began to call, 'Sebastian! Sebastian!' and Eric felt compelled to point at the open door and peer out of it himself.

On that side street where only one lamp hung, casting all else into darkness, they saw the child sitting on the kerb, holding a puppy in his arms. Sometimes, when it struggled and yipped, he set it down where it snuffled among bits of paper, rags, empty cans. The child, too, got down into the drain so they could explore the debris together. The puppy had seized something it found particularly tasty – a shoe sole, perhaps, or a stained rag – and the child tried to tug it away. Both pulled and struggled. The child was laughing to feel the puppy's small, fierce strength and tried to match it.

Then both of Sebastian's parents converged on the pair and picked their son out of the drain. He kicked his legs and protested loudly but they kissed his cheeks and stroked his hair and carried him back into the inn.

Eric saw there was to be no more conversation tonight; he was to be left to turn things over in his mind as if they were cards in a game of solitaire and to watch the bustle in the kitchen gradually close down for the night.

By then he had drunk a whole bottle of red wine. That, on top of his exhaustion and the doubts and discomforts of a journey undertaken on a whim. So, when he finally went down to bed – down, down the stone stairwell, one pounding step after another, in semi-darkness, the last journey of the day – he felt his head, his brain, his mind come crashing down together. Bits and pieces, shreds and shards, all cluttered and confused and rattling as he threw himself on the bed. He lay against the red cushions, under the white wool rug, and tried to steady the swinging of his mind.

Usually it was steadying to think of Em, so he did. Although he had no idea how far along she was with *her* journey, he could be certain that wherever she was, she was Em. Down to the shadow of a disapproving frown on her brow as she observed him sprawling there, idle. It would creep across her face whenever she came back from a long day at the lab and found him at home, in Boston, listening to Mozart or to Schumann, with the cat Shakespeare ensconced on his lap and his book held slightly to the side. Her disapproval would never really cast a shadow on his mood which tended by nature to be halcyon; besides, it was more like a cool, grey cloud than a threatening storm. He would tell her of his day at the library, pass on amusing bits of information he had extracted from his reading and describe the scenes at the café where he had his tea and scone overlooking Harvard Square and from where he watched the tramps, the musicians, the chess players and students who provided it with movement and amusement. He carefully refrained from letting her know how bored he had been during those long hours at the library, how he could scarcely bear to look at the thesis he had written on immigration patterns in Boston in the 1900s and then proposed to expand, for lack of a fresh idea, into a study of immigration in general. He had received a generous grant to do so but that did not help to inspire him. Dispersing the particular into the general seemed to cast it far into space and his intention of pursuing it faltered and dwindled and threatened to fail. He would have gladly thrown it into the trash can at the door to the café and been rid of that last link to tiresome student days, but he was not prepared to confess this to Em. Her interest in his 'studies', perhaps a polite reciprocation of his interest in hers, was still of importance to him. It had astonished him, to begin with, that the young woman he had noticed for her somewhat aloof and preoccupied air, setting her apart from the groups crowding the hallways of their dormitory with their clutter and noise, could show such an interest in a subject and field other than her own. Yet she was willing to stroll with him across the campus to their classes, earnestly talking, and when he searched her out in the cafeteria, to eat her sandwich and her soup with him rather than with anyone else. He was to learn that it was Emily Hatter's gift to give her entire and serious attention to the subject at hand, so much so that it bolstered his own rather uncertain confidence in it. After their graduation, almost without any discussion about the matter, they moved into an apartment together and were not surprised to find the arrangement entirely comfortable, even Em's cat adjusting to it without protest. (The idea of 'shelter' often came to Eric's mind even if he never spoke of it.) After a day spent in separate academic pursuits, they would come together to cook a dish of pasta and make a salad and eat to the melodious outflow of sound from piano, horn and clarinet, compositions that seemed to express their own harmony. Even the crease between Em's even eyebrows would gradually soften and smooth over. They seemed already to have arrived at a stage that many couples require thirty years to achieve, although both were still graduate students and had not spoken once of marriage; there was often an atmosphere of self-congratulation hovering over these perfect occasions.

It was not his increasing loss of faith in his own studies that finally upset the safely even keel and security of their lives together in the apartment they shared in a red-brick block of student apartments on a street lined with many more such blocks. Unexpectedly, it was Em who announced one evening towards the end of a long, sorry winter that it was now unavoidable that she carry her research into 'the field'. Her field was the forests of Yucatán where mosquitoes teemed and malaria was rife. Boston had become too limited for her, she had outgrown its resources and needed to proceed.

That evening she sat quietly, running her fingers over and over again through her cropped hair – so fair as to seem almost ashen – committed to the next stage of her work but aware of its significance to their relationship. 'I'll be away in the field with my professors,' she kept explaining as if afraid he did not understand the implications. It appeared he did not because, instead of turning apprehensive or worried as she expected him to be at the announcement of her departure, he seemed stirred and excited by the news. 'But, Em, it'll be just the thing for me,' was his unexpected response, in a voice that had risen by several decibels, and with his spectacles flashing his enthusiasm. 'You know how stuck I am for ideas.'

She had not known. 'What do you mean?'

'Oh, I've done all the work on that thesis I ever wanted to do. I haven't really the least interest in taking it any further –'

'But your fellowship? You were given it to work on a book.'

'I just can't – you see, I haven't the right kind of mind for theory. I've always worked with detail, Em. And I can't seem to find the one I need.'

'Have you spoken about this to your professors?'

'No, no, not yet. But I've considered making a fresh proposal.'

'Have you? You never told me about it.'

'No, well, I haven't any fresh ideas yet,' he confessed, 'but if I came with you to Mexico, I'm sure ideas would just come *flooding* in,' and he smiled as winningly, as persuasively, as he could, refusing to be discouraged by the doubt in her grey eyes.

As she ran her fingers nervously through her hair, he ran his through Shakespeare's.

Outside, Boston lay like a lumberyard, incapacitated by winter, knee-deep in slush, ice and mud, its houses sagging under their sodden weight. Gutters awry, window frames mouldy, wood piles and metal junk protruding from the soiled snow. As if to emphasise its plight, a branch of the bare tree at the window cracked and plunged downwards with its burden of ice. One glance through the curtains – he could never get them to meet – at the traffic crawling in the street below, and Eric resumed his pleas.

'I might come across – um, something in Mexico that

would put me on the right track,' he said in what he hoped was a confident tone.

'Or not. You don't know Mexico, you've never been there, it might not prove the right place at all. You're an Americanist after all.' Em could not see how her Mexico, and its mosquitoes, could possibly provide him with ideas for a book on American immigration.

But in the subsequent months of preparation for the field study, it became clear that Em would be away in Mexico for a considerable amount of time, and she began to give way to Eric's persuasions; they found themselves discussing such details as where Shakespeare was to be housed in their absence and arranging to take him to Eric's parents before they left.

Visits to Eric's family were always hasty, improvised, scrambled affairs, infrequent and rarely satisfactory. Em, who came from a solid phalanx of doctors, dentists, optometrists and surgeons in Philadelphia and its environs, so that her own choice of a medical profession seemed not only logical but inevitable, never could find such a link between the Eric she knew and his family which was, effectively, his mother's side of it.

There they were, all over the great muddy yard by the sea, at one end the fish shop and at the other the restaurant that carried the family name, O'Brien's, on its great wooden signboard with its painted image of a fiery-red lobster, and down below the docks where the boats drew up with the daily catch. The collection of white clapboard houses they lived in were scattered up and down the slope of granite with its crown of tough, stunted fir trees at the top. In one, dogs barked, in another babies squalled, smoke billowed from the chimney of a third and laundry flapped on a line outside a fourth. Men and women dressed identically in blue jeans, plaid flannel shirts and gum boots climbed up and down between them, bearing lobster pots and tubs of fish or dragging lengths of fish netting. Some were setting out in their boats, others returning. The smells of diesel oil from boat engines, of fish from the sea, of brine and seaweed, swirled as thick as steam in the chill autumnal air, and gulls hovered, shrieking with unappeased greed.

Em hung back, letting Eric go before to find his parents within the crowding clan. How could he, her Eric – scholarly and spectacled – have emerged from out of it? she wondered, as always. She held the cowering, apprehensive Shakespeare in his box in her arms, protectively, but it might have been Eric she was protecting.

He had explained to her, often, his parents' recognition of the awkwardness of having such a misfit for a son, this pale, frail scholar within a clan of hearty Maine fisherfolk. Eric's father had always gamely accepted the blame, as an Englishman and an intruder on their Irish Catholic tribe, but it was his mother who had, in her direct and practical way, dealt with the problem by plucking him out of the turmoil of a high-spirited family bred for the outdoors, and sending him to a boarding school for an education. This went totally against the family tradition – it was not even a parochial school run by the Irish priests, which she might have chosen if she had wanted, and which would have been quite acceptable, but a small, progressive school run by an old school friend of hers from the convent school, who had rebelled against their own education and created an alternative in the hills of New Hampshire. Here they taught

Eric according to the precepts of Rudolf Steiner and after years of dancing barefoot to the music of a piano, painting with oils in airy studios, playing the flute and attending classes on wooded hilltops, he found himself totally unfit for life in the family's boatyards and fishing boats; lobster as food totally repelled him. The one direction he could take was to the universities and libraries of Cambridge, Massachusetts. Returning to the clan remained as daunting and bracing as a plunge into the Atlantic Ocean.

Not that anyone had the time to notice his trepidation, or Em's. Eric was directed to the back room of the restaurant where his father had an office and kept the books while Em went in search of Eric's mother. She was not to be found in her house, having communal duties to fulfil, but Shakespeare could be unboxed in the relative privacy it afforded before Em ventured into the restaurant where the clan were gathering for a meal now that it was closed to the public for the season. She and Eric sat on opposite sides of the long table and she glanced at him, quiet between his equally quiet father and a large and gregarious uncle. Then there was the clam chowder to attend to with the accompanying oyster crackers, and after that a procession of dishes each as large as a basin and oozing with sauces and gravies, melted butter and cream. 'You city folk need some feeding up,' she was told each time someone heaped another spoonful on her plate.

The talk ricocheted back and forth across the table, and she found she was not required to add to it. Eric had previously pointed out to her how no one in his family – other than his mother, privately – ever asked them a question about their own lives: where they lived or how, what they worked at, where they had been or what they planned to do; these were simply not subjects of any interest. Instead, as usual, they told and retold the same family stories, each time evoking the same responses. Em could hardly believe it but yes, once again they were telling the story that Eric so hated to hear, about the first time he went trick-or-treating as a child on Hallowe'en.

'You remember that mouse mask we gave you to wear, Eric –'

'The Mickey Mouse mask from the cereal box –'

'When you wanted to be Batman –'

'And you set off brave as a lion, with a pillowcase for candy, and when you got to the first house and saw all the pumpkins lined up with candles in them –'

'On a dark and windy night –'

'And then the door opened and this hu-uge clown with a red nose and carroty hair and great big grin painted on his face came out to give you some candy –'

'You just screamed and *ran*.'

'And the clown ran after you, yelling, "Here, take some candy," but you were so scared –'

'You never went trick-or-treating again with the rest of us.'

Em tried to catch Eric's eye but he was looking sideways, mumbling, 'Well, Hallowe'en *is* scary, you know.'

'It's meant to be!' they chorused. 'But clowns are not. Why were you scared by the *clown*?' Then they went on to talk of the time the circus had come to the neighbouring town and they had all been taken to it but Eric had disgraced himself by letting out a shriek when the clown appeared and was reduced to such a state that they had had to get up and leave. Groans rang out all around the table as at this point they always did.

Eric's mother, several seats away, sat quietly waiting till they were done with their stories and their dishes when she could rise and start clearing the table. Em joined her with relief.

At the kitchen sink the two women found themselves alone together, Eric's mother washing while Em dried. They had done this on previous vists too: the mother, being the only daughter in a family of sons, had this role to play. At the same time, she made it evident that while she cooked, cleaned and washed up for the others, she had a mind of her own, separate and intact. She had shown it when she had insisted on marrying the English stranger who appeared in their village some forty-odd years ago, and again when she chose to send Eric away to school. Now Em, wiping plate after plate with a dish towel, saw another diplay of it: a steady stream of questions was being directed at her, regarding her work, her research, her university, its labs, her colleagues and her workplace by the woman who had rarely left the fishing village in Maine where she had been born but seemed keenly aware – unlike the rest of her family – that there was a world beyond it. Em, scrubbing and polishing furiously with her dish towel, tried to make satisfying answers while attempting to comprehend a mind so free of resentment or envy, so buoyant with curiosity and quest.

When the last dish was put away and the towel hung up to dry, they paused for a bit by the sink, looking out through the window made almost opaque with steam at the rocks below, where the figures of Eric and his father could just be discerned, picking their way gingerly around rock pools and boulders. It was clearly the two of them, the only men who wore neither plaid flannel shirts nor gum boots. Hands deep in the pockets of their black parkas, the hoods pulled up over their heads which were lowered to the spray that flew up from the white-capped waves of the wintry sea.

Eric's mother gave a little laugh and dabbed her finger at the window pane, making an opening in the steamy screen. 'Don't they look just like a pair of herons?' she said to Em, as if she thought them a pair of exotic visitors to her workaday world which, perhaps, Em did too.

Driving back to Boston in the early dark, Em and Eric were both silent with fatigue and with their thoughts. Em did finally stir herself to say, 'Your dad was quiet.'

'Isn't he always?'

'Your mom's family seems to overwhelm him.'

'Oh, he likes that. They leave him alone, in his office room, with his books. Did you get any time with Mom?'

'We did the dishes together.'

'Talk?'

'I did more than her.'

'It's not her thing.'

Em laughed suddenly. 'She did say you looked like a pair of herons down on the rocks, you and your dad. And you did. I wish I had come with you.'

He put out his hand to clasp hers for saying that. 'I wish you had.' They were passing a row of stores and their attendant parking lots, gas stations and motels, with the traffic and the glare of lights making it difficult to talk and drive at the same time. It was when they achieved a quieter, darker stretch of the highway with tall fir forests looming on either side that he gave her some information he had clearly been mulling over. 'When I told Dad we were going to Mexico, he told me something I hadn't known before – that he was born there. He'd never told me that.'

'But how strange, Eric – not to *know* where your dad was born!'

'Well, you know my family *is* strange. You've always said that,' he teased her.

'But as strange as that! I never guessed. Why *hadn't* he told you before?'

'I suppose because he doesn't remember a thing about it. He was taken to England as an infant and brought up there. Mexico is just a fairy tale to him.'

'Oh,' Em yawned. There seemed no point in pursuing a conversation that had no substance. She settled deeper into the seat, putting her head back to sleep while Eric drove.

Chapter 2

I dreamed of Mexico and I am in Mexico: the move
from the first state to the second happened in these
conditions without the slightest shock . . . for me never
before has reality fulfilled with such splendour the
promise of dreams.

André Breton, 1938

Em's doubts about letting Eric accompany her appeared
well founded as soon as they stepped up into the plane
together with her colleagues, two terribly sober and
certain men who talked between themselves constantly,
using a language Eric could not follow, it was so specialised
and technical. He had followed them in, dressed for a
holiday in a warm climate, and found himself with nothing
to say. He had convinced himself that scientists were fascinating people: they knew the human being and the
phenomenon of life as no one else did, after all. He had
imagined he would put intelligent questions to them, and
listen to their stories of medical emergencies, crises and
curiosities. But they had no stories, they were not doctors:
they did research. If they saw patients, they saw only those
parts necessary to their research and were not in the least
interested in anything beyond these bounds. Of course,
what Em shared with them was precisely that focus, that

intense and exclusive focus, and it was what Eric had hoped to escape on concluding his thesis in order to let a wider, more expansive view take over and transform his world. Realising he would have to embark on that journey alone, he thought it best to leave them to themselves and fell back. They had glanced at his initially hopeful, ingratiating smile, ignored it, and gone ahead.

He insisted they take the three seats in front together, sat behind them and read all the airline magazines, drank all the drinks offered him and listened to the animated conversation in Spanish between members of a family scattered through several rows of seats while they passed the smaller ones from lap to lap along with bottles of milk and pacifiers and diaper bags, toys and snack packs. He began to get a headache from the chatter and the glare that came in through the window as the plane droned its way over endless, colourless plains and the pleats and convolutions of mountains that were like prints left by giant knuckles in a pan of putty-coloured dough.

The headache was blown out of his head when the top of Popocatépetl suddenly floated into sight, disembodied in the haze over Mexico City, catching him utterly by surprise. No one had told him he would see Popocatépetl but he knew it could be nothing else, nothing less. 'Em,' he shouted, rising in his seat to tap her head in front of him, 'Em, look!' as if he were a boy, her boy.

But Em and her colleagues had visited Mexico many times before; they glanced out of the window, took note of the familiar landmark and what they saw had the effect only of making them gather up their files and briefcases and begin to prepare for the descent. Eric was left with his face flattened against the oval aperture to catch what he could of the magic of a cone of ice floating in a blur of clouds and dust over a dun cityscape.

The disjointedness of their joint experience of Mexico was repeated at every step. While Em and her colleagues passed casually through the immigration barriers and collected their baggage with the harassed air of professional business travellers, Eric found himself distracted by everything in the airport – the kiosks displaying textiles bright with rainbow stripes and rainbow flowers, tequila bottles shaped like cacti, sweets made out of cacti and fruit, and the arrivals hall which was swamped by more people with black hair and brown skin than he had ever encountered before, families embracing and weeping and laughing as if they lived their lives on the level of grand opera. Outside, he was faced with light that struck more whitely, electrically than he had ever seen on to a spectrum of colour unknown in Boston, Massachusetts – flat-roofed houses with pink and orange and violet walls, pea-green taxis and leaf-green buses. When they reached the hotel where the tranquilising effect of plashing water in marble fountains was cancelled by the shrieking of birds of bright plumage in tall cages, he had to lie down, he felt the blood racing in his veins too fast. Em did not appear concerned; she went about unpacking, hanging clothes in a gigantic armoire and putting out her jars and bottles on shelves of glass and marble, saying merely, 'It's the altitude. It affects some people that way' – not her, of course.

Later that evening, they took the elevator of intricate art nouveau filigree up to the rooftop restaurant and sat by the balustrade with their drinks, looking down on to the plaza that seemed built on a scale greater than a merely human one; it struck Eric as strange in a country where the human scale was generally small. Over this great field of volcanic rock from the ruins of the Aztec temples, the tricolour of Mexico whipped like a dragon in the wind from the mountains that ringed the city and were visible at the end of every avenue and street, benevolent and protective witches wrapped in dark skirts. Eric and Em were just in time to observe the ceremony of taking down the flag for the night by a platoon of toy-sized soldiers as stiff and smart as painted lead. The figures strolling across the vast expanse with their silver balloons might have been toys, too, fashioned for the gods. Lights were coming on haphazardly, so many embers in the soot and coal of the night.

'Em, you never told me it would be like this,' Eric said, tearing his eyes away from the scene to her at last. She had never seemed so pale, so Nordic as here, with her grey eyes, her fair hair and her white dress.

Instead of seeming pleased with his response to the scene to which she had brought him, Em appeared to grow more apprehensive. She frowned slightly and said, 'But what will you *do* here, Eric?'

'What do you mean?'

'I mean, while I am away.'

Eric had been picking up grains of salt from the rim of his margarita glass; now he licked them and looked at the oversized goblet with its blue rim and its wedge of lime and crust of salt as if it were an object in a museum, requiring his serious attention and measured opinion. He was considering, too, the fact already known to him, of course, that Em would be going away with her colleagues to carry on their research 'in the field'. He knew it would be foolish to tag along, that it was not for him, he would be in the

way, but somehow he had neglected to give this fact sufficient thought. Of course, in Boston they worked sepa-
rately too, coming together in the evenings to cook their
pasta and listen to Mozart or to Schumann. He was quite
capable of spending the day alone even if Em seemed to
need reassurance on this point and would anxiously ask,
'Did you get any work done today? Did you start with the
book?' He would protest, 'But, Em, writing is not a nine-
to-five job in the city. One doesn't just sit at a desk and
type one's ten pages a day, you know.' Now he began to
doubt his ability to sit at a desk and write two pages, or
one, while in this giddy state with so much around to be
experienced and regarded. Nor had he thought about
where he would go or where he would stay in her absence.
He said the only thing that occurred to him at this moment
of pressure: 'D'you think I could come with you to
Yucatán?'

'Of course not,' she said immediately, and he looked
at her and smiled: it was what she would say and she
was quite right to do so, of course. How foolish to think
he could join the company of the sure and the certain,
those who knew what to do with themselves from
morning to night every day of the year and everywhere.
Had he not always been the misfit? It was his role; she
knew it.

'But don't you have any plans at all?' she asked, sounding worried and making the straw in her margarita glass
bob up and down to show it.

'Only the vaguest one, Em. I'm hoping it will become
clear. I have to wait for that "Eureka" moment.'

'Oh, Eric. I know what you'll do with yourself – stroll
around and chat.'

'That is what a writer does,' he smiled at her, he thought winningly.

This exchange, not at all atypical of their relationship, did not quite cast down Eric's spirits. Rabbit-like, these wriggled free from under it and went out to meet the city, a city that strewed its sights before him as a carpet-seller might his carpets, a jeweller his gems – the immense plaza where bird-shaped kites rose into the sky to meet the eagles circling there, the arcades alongside with their jewellery stores filled with gold ornaments of Mayan or Aztec design and guarded by armed police and police dogs on chains, the sweetmeat shops where the sweets resembled gems, the restaurants where waitresses floated in balloon-like skirts and wing-like caps, the pavement vendors outside proferring lottery tickets, safety pins, or songbirds in stacked cages, the Zapotec women from the country who spread out their bunches of dried herbs, their shrivelled scorpions and fried grasshoppers on little mats they rolled up and made disappear as soon as the city police roared up in white jeeps, the stalls where creams and lotions were sold in seashells and jumping beans jumped on trays; and, leading off from the plaza, the streets of the old quarter where there were stately mansions with blackened façades, drooping wrought-iron balconies, strings of laundry and leftover Christmas tinsel, and the dark rooms beyond from which television sets flickered with blue and violet images, intermittently lighting up the family groups gathered to watch the *telenovelas*; and the shops below which displayed white satin wedding gowns and wax orange-blossom tiaras for brides and little girls at their first communion, or ecclesiastical artefacts of purple and plum-coloured satin, and velvet skirts fringed with tinsel to drape around the heads of madonnas or round the lower regions of saints whose exposed hearts and wounds oozed crimson paint; or party gifts, masks and costumes from which you could choose to dress up as a zapatista or a witch; underwear shops with naughty knickers and lace socks, stalls selling household goods like tin and plastic buckets and pans and bowls . . . and down the street an old man would come, banging a great drum with one hand and blowing a brass trumpet held in the other, while at the corner outside the cathedral fleshy dancers in costumes of brilliant feathers and anklets of jangling bells danced and whirled the Aztec dances for tourists with cameras, purses and pesos.

Eric could not have enough of it. It was as though he had been starving throughout his northern existence and now, reborn a traveller, could feast and gourmandise without restraint till he was so replete that he had to sink down on to a bench in an *allée* of low and shady trees that undulated with flocks of glossy and loudly shrieking starlings, and ask himself if he should not be putting all this down on paper in a handy notebook that would swell with his insights and impressions and bring to Em's sober grey eyes a flicker of admiration or, at least, approval.

Then some wonderfully dark-eyed urchin would wander up with a shoebox strung over his shoulder and offer to give him a spectacular display of shoe-polishing skill, and how could he deny he was in need of that? So he would stretch out his legs and submit and find the exercise as blissfully soothing as a massage, so tilt his head back and fall into a reverie, seeing the white-icing-coated dome of the Palacio de Bellas Artes upside down and the fountains spouting downwards into beds of scarlet flowers, and think the scene, the setting, sufficient in itself: why would anyone ask for more than simply to observe, imbibe?

Of course, that very question would summon up the dark frown on Em's clear brow like the brown haze issuing from the lanes of crawling traffic on either side of the Alameda Park. He would empty all his change into the shoeshine boy's palm, rise from the bench, turn his back on the city's architectural and occupational excesses, and walk off, chewing his underlip and wondering how to assuage and erase that frown so that the city could once again become the Ali Baba's cave of curiosities it had been.

So it had been serendipitous that, while browsing through the bookshop of a cultural centre in the Colonia Roma on a somnolent afternoon, he had seen a notice pinned up announcing a lecture to be given by a woman with a Teutonic name, on the Huichol Indians and their belief in the powers of the peyote cactus, to be followed by cocktails in the garden conveniently laid outside the bookshop. Of course, he lingered on for the event, preferring that to returning to the empty hotel room and waiting for Em while hanging over the balcony rail and displaying the capacity for enjoying idleness that she so deplored.

The small circular auditorium under a gilt and painted ceiling that might have done credit to a baroque chapel was full, and Eric, at the door, stood looking at the way the afternoon light streamed from the skylights on to all the expectant faces. Many of them were obviously American or European, and many he could not identify as one or the other. He knew by now that in Mexico all foreigners took to dressing flamboyantly, in vivid blues and scarlets, with heavy embroidery and broad belts, and to wearing a great deal of elaborate jewellery. He became aware that the audience was made up almost entirely of women. Was it because the lecturer was a woman, he wondered, or that men were at work at this time of day? The few who were present did not look as if they ever worked; their assurance and elegance were impeccable. Eric slid on to a vacant chair next to one, he hoped unobtrusively.

When the lecturer appeared on the stage, held up at the elbow by a younger woman whose task it was to introduce her, what was immediately noticeable were her air of authority and what was, even for this gathering, an extraordinarily extravagant costume. She was draped in Indian garments, striped and flowered, trimmed and embroidered, red and green and blue and yellow like the feathers of a macaw, and silver jewellery from her neck to her knees. Her head was long, elongated like the skulls one saw in museums depicting various forms of torture undertaken for the sake of achieving a particular ideal of beauty, now more likely to be considered grotesque. Its upper portion was swathed in a silk turban fastened with a great brooch of Mayan, or Aztec, design. Under it, the eyelids drooped like a weary hound's and were painted a deep purple.

The younger woman assisted her to a seat as if she were an object of great price and fragility, then turned to give a dazzling smile followed by a sparkling talk in what was, unfortunately for Eric, Spanish. He could only sit back with folded arms and admire her – a type of Mexican woman who seemed to him the epitome of elegance and beauty with a vivacious manner to match. Eric studied her from the top of her glossy head to the tips of her very high heels and could not help a smile at the thought of this paragon of feminity beside his sober Em: what would they have made of each other?

By the time she concluded her introduction with a flutter of her manicured hands and a flash of their silver tips, Eric had come to no convincing answer to that question. But now the fantastic dame on her carved throne began to speak, and although it was a shocking transition from the grace and attractiveness of the one woman to the deliberate eccentricity of the other, the latter commanded no less attention. If anything, she commanded rather more because in addition to her bizarre appearance, she had a voice so low and deep that it forced one to lean forward and strain to catch her every word till one grew accustomed to its peculiar register, slightly hoarse and rasping.

This took Eric several minutes and then the mixture of several languages and vocabularies that she employed caused an even further delay before he could conclude that her lecture was, in the main, in Spanish too. He now regretted his minimal acquaintance with the language. The pronounced accent she brought to it caused further confusion. Eric gave himself up to riding its waves or, rather, floundering in them.

And then something unexpected happened. Eric was later to describe the experience, to Em, as like stumbling into a rabbit hole – falling, falling, he said, till all was a welter of strange words, strange names churning around him. Then, with a bump, landing upon the startling awareness that many of them were actually familiar to him. It was like being in a crowd of swiftly moving strangers and finding that there were faces among them that you recognised. Or like walking, with difficulty, through a bed of gravel and coming across veins of liquid brightness running through it. Golden, dramatic words unfurling through the rubble, words like Sierra Madre

Oriental, Sierra de los Catorce, Real del Monte, La Purísima, La Asunción, Los Lorenzos, La Luz, Valenciana . . . and he had heard them before; each had an image, a memory linked to it that he struggled to resurrect. It was as if they were the words of a song he used to know, or had heard sung. His mind scrambled, as if on its knees, to recover the images they had once conjured.

Strangely, the images were not of gold or silver, rocks, canyons or mountains – but of the tiled surround of a fireplace in an English cottage, and brasses and chintzes, china and tapestry. The colours were dull; brown dominated, orange intruded. At the window great clouds of moisture were being flung with the sound of pebbles, or gravel – rain, together with the waves of the sea.

But indoors a fire was lit, and it shone on the bald pate of a small, neat man in a brown wool cardigan with brown leather patches at the elbows. He was waving about the pipe he had been smoking as he talked to Eric about places with the same mellifluous names, about mines where he had supervised the bringing up of ore to the surface through shafts sunk into the mountain, and how it was treated till the precious stuff was separated from the dirt. He took down from the mantelpiece, from behind the silver-framed photographs of family weddings and christenings, a little replica of a string of railway wagons filled with tiny pieces of glittering metal. 'Is that gold?' the child Eric asked, in awe. 'Is that gold, Grandad?' with his knees digging into the nubbly wool of the rug by the fire. The old man rubbed the glinting fragments and chuckled. "Course it is, boy, 'course it is.' Just then a tall and grey-haired woman in a pink cardigan came out of the kitchen holding a teapot that wore a knitted skirt and a flowered bonnet on its knob, and said, 'Don't fill his head with that nonsense, Davey. We don't want him running off to the back of beyond to look for the pot of gold at the end of a rainbow like you did.'

'Oh, he wouldn't do that, Madge, and I didn't either. I found it at the end of a mine shaft, in the ground,' Grandad said, and began to recite the names of the mines from where the fabulous stuff had come – La Luz, Valenciana, Los Lorenzos, Real del Monte, Real de Catorce, Sierra Madre Oriental – words that made the boy tingle as if the pins and needles in his knees had spread all through him while he knelt there, listening. 'Again, Grandad, tell me again!' he cried, but the woman was cross, saying, 'Now, see, you've got him all wound up and he won't go to bed.' She made him put away the little toy train – it vanished behind the framed photographs, the brides and the babies drew their wedding and christening gowns over it – and Eric never saw it again. Teacups were filled – with milk for Eric – and at the window the clouds and the waves hurled themselves, beating and drowning out the golden names and images.

But now, this evening, they were resurrected by the improbable creature on the podium in front of a gathering of the Centre for Anthropological and Ethnographic Studies. Eric had not thought about them in years, never having gone back to his father's English home or seen his grandparents since that one, early visit. When they died, his father had gone alone to their funerals in a churchyard in the deep, narrow valley in Cornwall where he had grown up. He had spoken of it rarely, whether because he had memories that pained him or because of his natural reticence, Eric could not tell. He had brought back a small box with a few objects but immediately put it away in the attic and not reopened it. Perhaps memories and nostalgia had to be abandoned, like excess baggage, if one was to complete the experience his father had had of emigration and a new beginning in a New World.

It occurred to him that he should take down some of the names so that he could – now grown, literate – look them up on a map and try to unearth the connections, burrow through a tunnel back into the old country to the old man and his toys in the seaside cottage with the rug on which he'd knelt by the fire, tingling. He began to pat down his pockets in search of paper and pencil. As he did so, he became distracted by a murmur that was rippling through the audience. Curious, he started to cast glances around and found a subdued but unmistakable air of consternation. Instead of listening to the grande dame, people were turning to each other with raised eyebrows, and whispering. She herself seemed not to notice this change in the atmosphere of the room, or if she did, she ignored it; in fact, she raised her voice slightly as she went on to the end of her talk, then indicated that she wanted to rise from her seat and leave without inviting questions.

Released, the audience streamed out on to a terrace lined with immense terracotta urns in which orange trees displayed, in the Mexican way, both flowers and fruit together. At one end a table was laid with white linen and set with platters and pitchers and glasses of food and wine. Helping himself to both, Eric looked around, smiling, in the hope of finding someone who looked willing to answer his questions. The gorgeous young woman who had introduced the speaker was already surrounded by people and was talking to them with great rapidity, gesturing with her long hands and fine fingers; it was clear he was not the only one with questions. He did not feel he could approach her at this fraught moment and turned away, a glass of wine in one hand and a plate in the other, to survey the scene now cast into shadow by the ornately moulded stucco of the cultural centre and its exquisite dome.

Catching the eye of the white-haired gentleman who had been his neighbour in the auditorium, and who was standing beside a woman with fine-spun grey hair and jewels so massive as to make her look fragile by comparison, he strolled over to them to see if they could enlighten him. 'Well, that was quite an exciting talk, wasn't it?' he asked, hoping he did not seem too intrusive.

But he had made the right conjecture because the gentleman replied readily, in English. 'About its exciting quality, I cannot say, but it certainly contained an element of surprise.'

Eric, still curious, waited for an explanation.

'To come to hear a talk on the Huichol and the significance of the peyote cactus in their rituals, then hear instead an attack on the mining industry was definitely a surprise.'

His companion said something now so sharply that it too caused consternation, and Eric had no alternative but to confess his ignorance of Spanish. Translating this for the lady who nodded the towering arrangement of spidery grey hair on her head and gave a pinched smile as if her worst suspicions had been confirmed, the elderly gentleman explained to Eric, 'Doña Vera is connected – through marriage – to a prominent family whose share in the mining industry is well known but it is the first time, as far as we know, that she has spoken of it in public.'

'Ha!' Eric exclaimed, beginning to see. 'Did she speak specifically of this family and the mines they own?'

'No, no, no, not at all. She explained why she chose today not to speak of the Huichol beliefs and customs but instead of the industry that destroyed their habitat and made it difficult to continue their traditions such as the pilgrimage and the hunt for peyote. But she was speaking to an audience that is informed, academic, specialist –' he licked the words as if they were tiny crystals on his lips – 'certainly not industrialists or businessmen, so we are all surprised, you might say.'

The woman at his side spoke to him again, with asperity, and he replied to her out of the corner of his mouth, then took her elbow and turned away from Eric in search of a group with whom conversation might flow more freely.

Eric helped himself to more hors d'oeuvres. If Em were here, he thought, she would have understood and grasped the whole situation in no time.

The little hors d'oeuvres were delicious, but the thought of Em made him deposit his plate and glass and make his way towards the wrought-iron gate that opened on to the street. As he did so, he passed the bookshop where he had begun the evening and saw the lecturer seated there with a plate on her lap and a cup in her hand. Several people hovered around her, conversing in respectful tones, but she herself was occupied in devouring a large cream cake. A bit of the cream adhered to her upper lip and as Eric slouched past on his way to the gate, he could not help thinking she looked like an aged and very spoilt cat being fed by her devoted keepers for whom she has the utmost disdain.

Making his way back to the hotel through the crowds, Eric for once found no distraction in the food stalls where pepper flakes spluttered in hot oil, and office workers paused for a snack on their way home, or the sharp young men peddling designer watches, bottled perfumes and pornographic comic books. Instead, he was trying intently to pursue those words and names heard twenty-odd years ago in a cottage in Cornwall that had now reappeared only to escape and flee from him like so many goldfish darting into the turbid waters of Mexico City's evening streets.

He tried to capture the links and present them to Em like the trophies they were to him while she packed in readiness for an early flight next day to Mérida, but she seemed not to be listening with her usual attentiveness. Barefoot, clad only in a brief petticoat, her hair in wet wisps from a recent shampoo, she went about her packing with a preoccupied air.

'Well, if it's true that your grandfather was a miner in Mexico once you surely couldn't have forgotten that, could you?' she asked, a little exasperated because he was in her way as she went back and forth between the suitcase open on her bed and the brushes, combs, bottles, jars and still damp pieces of clothing that were scattered about the room. What with packing, an ending and a beginning, she was distracted.

'Well, I had,' Eric insisted. 'I *had* because I saw him on just that one visit. People didn't fly back and forth across the pond the way they do now, and that's the only time my dad took me to England. He left me in Cornwall and took my mother off on a motor trip through the old country, or something of the sort, I don't know, I was five, maybe four years old. I must have been too young to take along, I suppose. I really haven't any other memories of the visit – just that one.'

'But surely you'd have heard you dad *speaking* of his father? Didn't he say anything the time he told you he was *born* in Mexico?'

'Not really,' Eric said. He was lying now against the pillows and absently running his fingers through the vines and tendrils carved into the mahogany forest of the bedstead, moodily giving thought to things he had not previously given any. 'He did tell me there were some letters I could look at when I wanted, letters his mother wrote home to Cornwall.'

Em stopped her constant movement between bags and boxes, bed and armoire, and stood with a pile of fresh laundry in her arms. 'Couldn't you ask him for them?'

'I could,' Eric agreed. 'I will. I think his mother died here because he told me another thing I hadn't known: the woman I met in Cornwall when I was a child, she was *not* his mother, she was his stepmother.'

'Well, you English –' Em said, going back to her packing. 'No one ever knows what goes on in your families.'

He was angered suddenly and sat up. 'You know I've never even lived there, and *he* left the country himself. But now that I'm here, perhaps I can find out more.'

'That'll be interesting,' she said as if she were encouraging a child to run out and play.

He kicked aside her shoe bag and marched across to the window to open the shutters. 'This could be just what I need – for my book,' he announced, letting in the view of the plaza and the evening sky above it. He expected this reference to his 'book' to make an impression on her if nothing else did. 'I'd never thought my family could

38

ever be of help – but they might have something to give. I'll have to find out.'

Em stopped folding clothes into her case and said, crisply, 'Why don't you do just that?'

This led to what was an evening of almost total silence and disappointment. They were to have made a special occasion of that night since it was to be their last together for a while. Instead they cancelled their reservation at the Café Tacubaya and ate in the sepulchral hotel dining room watched over by waiters in funereal uniforms, and talking, if at all, of travel agencies and banks and postal services; then they retired to lie at opposite sides of the so-called 'matrimonial' bed, pretending to sleep till Em rose quietly at dawn to leave, and Eric, wide awake, watched her in the semi-dark.

He found he could not let her slip away without a word. Sitting up in a swaddle of bedclothes, he put out his arms and embraced her. 'Oh, Em,' he said, 'dear Em. Don't go.'

She leaned into him, stroking his hair, trying to calm the anguish she sensed in him and to some extent felt herself. 'It'll be all right,' she whispered.

'How? How?' he asked, pressing his face into her.

'You'll see,' she said, more firmly, putting her hands on his shoulders and pressing him away. 'When you're with me, you're – we are – too close. When you're by yourself, you'll find so much more than you would with me –'

'That's not so, Em,' he argued, trying to make out her expression in the pallid light of daybreak.

'You'll see, you'll see, it'll happen,' she said, trying to reassure him, and twisted gently out of his grasp, lifted her case and turned towards the door.

Chapter 3

When at the beginning of the sixteenth century the Spaniards landed in Mexico, they first met with the natives of Sempollan, not far from the sea . . . the chiefs wore silver and gold ornaments that attracted the rapacious glances of the white adventurers. Their first question was 'Whence comes this?' The natives pointed to the west. When, soon after, the ambassadors of Montezuma brought rich presents of the precious metals, adorned with emeralds, in order to induce the unbidden guests to turn back, they were confirmed in their opinion that there were literally golden mountains in the interior, and the cry was 'Forwards!'

Carl Sartorius, *Mexico and the Mexicans*, 1859

Painfully, creakily dismounting from the train at Matehuala, as mottled as a moth with the grime and soot of the journey, Eric enquired about transport to take him into the Sierra Madre Oriental that he had been making his way towards with decreasing hope and ambition. The driver of a truck heard him forlornly voice his destination and unexpectedly offered a ride. He had only to pick up a sick dog at a veterinarian's, he said, and then he would be on his way. Barely refreshed by a warm and rather flat soda bought at a kiosk, Eric climbed into the seat next to the driver. He had a moment of terror when the truck veered off the paved road and bumped its way over the desert to what looked like an abandoned shack, certain he was being kidnapped and would be robbed. But instead a young woman in a white lab coat came out with a limp and dispirited animal in her arms and helped the driver lift it into the truck, then smiled and waved goodbye. Now they set off on a highway that was drawn with the precision of a geometric diagram over the rubble of worn and ground-down hills, rattling over cobbles the shape and size of human skulls. The only other sight along the journey was an occasional giant maguey reaching its thorn-tipped leaves into the evenly metallic sky above. There was no sign of their destination; in every direction the dark stony land stretched out, the stands of maguey rising as stiff and grey as the stones themselves, and over it the sky and the light, both so immense that it did not seem there would ever be an end to them.

This was no longer the Mexico of colour and romance, Eric noted, and yet its emptiness and petrifaction were undeniably Mexican too.

Hearing Eric sigh in spite of himself with weariness and hopelessness, the truck driver glanced sympathetically and pointed his finger through the smeared and dusty windscreen. '*Allá arriba*,' he said, '*la Hacienda de la Soledad*.'

Eric straightened up to peer where he pointed. He could see neither roof nor homestead, nor believe that anyone could, or would, live on this desolate altiplano. But as they drew close enough to make out the first range of bullet-coloured mountains, a crater suddenly opened up in the earth as if a meteor had fallen and formed it; a wide, basin-like depression appeared which had not been visible from a distance. Around a still sheet of apparently

41

shallow water, dry *yacaté* grass waved and susurrated, responding to a breeze so imperceptible that nothing less delicate or sensitive could have detected it. There were a few desiccated mesquite trees on its bank and the more graceful, drooping pirul. Egrets and herons stood stock-still in the shallows as if they were roots or branches anchored to the clay below. Everything seemed fossilised except for the ripple of light that ran through the scene as it might in a mirage.

On the other side of the lake, against the flank of the mountain, there was a long, low building of stone, on three sides surrounded by an adobe wall that blended in so perfectly with the land that it could easily have been overlooked.

As they rounded the lake and drew closer, Eric made out horses in a corral below the hacienda, unexpectedly alive and mobile.

'*That* is where Doña Vera lives?' he murmured, more to himself than to his companion. 'It is – incredible.' Of course: just as Doña Vera herself had been incredible.

The driver laughed, pleased with the effect it had on his passenger, and changed gears with a triumphant shriek as he turned on to a dusty track that ascended the mountainside at an angle from the highway. It brought them round to the entrance of the hacienda set in the adobe wall. He looked both amused and sympathetic as he handed Eric's bag to him and let him off. '*Hasta luego*,' he called, and the bandaged dog, suddenly revived, sat up and echoed him with two short barks. Then they turned back to the highway, the truck taking to the silence as a jackhammer to stone.

Eric used a knocker shaped like a woman's hand, its

tapering fingers holding a brass ball that beat upon the worn wooden panel. When a maid limped up to let him in, he felt duly apologetic, saying, 'I had booked a room here, were you expecting me?' At her uncomprehending look, he decided to try another tack and simply ask, 'Is Doña Vera in?'

No, he was told by a shake of the head, and after he had taken in his bag and deposited it on the tiled floor of the entrance hall, he wandered out to wait for her in the great courtyard formed by the three wings of the house. In its centre was a fountain with a twinned pair of stone dolphins spouting into mossy jars. Beyond it, the land sloped down towards the corral. Chairs were set out under a feathery-leafed tree on that slope. He strolled down to it and stood looking, from a new angle, at the depression below filled with bleached grasses and still water. The sun was going down behind the mountain at his back and its shadow was slanting across the valley he had driven over to arrive here.

He stood with his hands on his hips, looking down at the horses in the corral pawing the earth and rubbing their flanks against the wooden fence in a blur of dust and chaff. Then, breasting the tall grasses like a swimmer emerging from a lake, another horse appeared; mounted on it was a slight shrunken figure he scarcely recognised from the salon in Mexico City. No longer the fantastically attired and theatrical creature she had appeared there, she was merely a small wiry figure in nondescript khaki who barely stood out in that over-whelming landscape. Yet there was no denying that in the way in which she appeared a natural part of the scene, she had made it her own, and Eric found himself

43

helplessly submitting to the notion of her as the mythical figure she was made out to be by those who knew her reputation.

A young boy came out of one of the tile-roofed stables by the corral and helped her dismount. They talked, patting the horse's neck and flanks and steadying the animal on its impossibly long legs and delicate hooves before it was led away. Now that Doña Vera was standing on solid ground, dressed in jodhpurs and boots, her white hair tucked under a hat, she seemed so much less formidable a being that Eric dared to step out from the shadow of the tree so she could see him.

Coming up the path between the crackling grasses, holding them aside with her whip, she called, 'Have you brought pastries?'

Eric, taken aback, not aware that he was supposed to have brought pastries, raised his hand to smooth down his hair as he always did when embarrassed, and mumbled, 'Umm, no – I'm sorry –'

She shot him an irritated look as she walked past, switching her whip. Eric reminded her that he had telephoned to request accommodation which he had been told was available at her hacienda.

'Why?' she asked, sharp as a crack of the whip in her hand.

He struggled to form an answer. Clearly, she was demanding one that lived up to her standards and expectations. And they were so high, she seemed to say by lifting her nose into the air and looking down it at him. Just then a maid came out of the house towards the tree and the garden chairs with a glass of lemonade on a tray; she was followed by a flock of small pug dogs, tripping along hurriedly on their toes and yipping with excitement at seeing their mistress.

Doña Vera scooped up one in her arms and seated herself. Accepting the glass of lemonade, she drank thirstily, keeping the glass away from the eager, wanting pug, and did not seem to think it at all necessary to ask Eric either to sit or drink too. The little dog leaping about her face, tickling her chin with its velvet folds, made her laugh delightedly and spill some of the lemonade down her front.

Knowing himself entirely irrelevant to the scene, Eric tried to explain. 'I heard your lecture in Mexico City last week, you see –'

She allowed herself to be distracted from her pleasures, although with irritation. 'You have an interest in an-thro-pol-ogy? In the Huichol Indian?'

Eric could only lie to be polite and avoid inflicting pain, not for any boastful reason. 'Not really,' he muttered, hoping the yipping of the pugs would drown out his craven response. He found himself actually shuffling his shoes. Now, if he had been the deliveryman of a patisserie, he thought ruefully. Instead, he had to admit, 'It's for a personal reason . . .'

But she had already decided he was of no interest and no importance. Rising from her chair with one pug in her arms, the others milling at her feet, she started towards the house, calling over her shoulder, 'Here, we conduct se-rious studies, señor.'

He watched the entourage as it turned its back on him and made its way to the house. Above, the pale disc of the sun had slid over the ridge of the mountain, and below, the grassy basin had filled up with darkness. Only the lake, a tarnished mirror, reflected whatever light remained in the sky, dully.

Unenthusiastically, he followed the grande dame and her retinue of masked miniatures at a safe distance, and saw that up and down the length of the corridors, lanterns of perforated tin had been lit, casting more shadow than light. Doña Vera must have given some instructions because the limping maid came out and picked up his bag and conducted him to a room at the end of a long corridor. From the sounds that reached him, it appeared that preparations were being made for dinner. Perhaps he could have a bath beforehand. Turning on a tap to fill the rusty tub in the tiled bathroom, he asked himself dejectedly why he had made the error of stopping at her malevolent establishment and not gone straight up the mountain to the mines. He lay back in the tepid water, floating in doubt, till the dinner gong boomed.

Going through the crepuscular entrance hall to the dining room with its single refectory table under a chandelier made of stags' antlers – many stags' antlers – he found most of the seats already taken, so he had to sit at a long distance from the head where Doña Vera presided. He was irked and relieved at the same time: sitting closer to her might have been rather like being close to a coiled serpent but, after all, he had come this long way to have conversation with her and could not afford to be the timid mouse now.

Glancing up and down the length of the table, he saw that most of the guests were very young, practically children, and from the talk that was flying around in a carefree, even oblivious fashion, they appeared to be students from American universities, universities in the western states, he guessed. This was surely not the company Doña Vera had chosen for herself. It must have to do with her turning the hacienda into a centre for 'serious' studies, and she must surely have her doubts, at such times, regarding her generosity. His ears ached already. It had been some years since he was an eager undergraduate. He hoped Doña Vera would appreciate that. He began to spoon up his soup from the bowl placed before him and felt it beneath him to join the chatter.

As he ate his soup, deliberately avoiding eye contact with the diners in front and to either side of him, he became aware that there were other totally silent guests present at the table. At the very foot of it, leaving a few seats vacant between them and the rest of the company, sat an Indian who was, in every way, not only physically and in dress, different from anyone else at the table, awkward with his hands and expression. After a while, another man, younger but dressed in the same fanciful costume as he – embroidered, beaded and beribboned – came and slipped quietly into a chair beside him; so did a woman with long plaits and a colourfully embroidered blouse. They occupied the three seats at the foot of the table, murmuring quietly to each other as they ate, resolutely avoiding looking at anyone else.

Eric tried not to be impolite but found himself glancing again and again at their costumes which seemed so at odds with the gravity of their manner, decorated as they were with the most vivid colours and a variety of motifs – butterflies, deer, snakes, flowers, peyote and maize. Each time he looked quickly away, equally embarrassed at not being able to speak to them and by the way no one else did either.

47

Yet up and down the table the talk appeared to be about 'the Huichol – peyote – Wirikúta – Hikuri' – words he had come to associate with just these people and for the study of whom Doña Vera had become renowned. Yet the three people about whom the talk revolved appeared not to be involved themselves, perhaps preferring to keep out of it. They talked only among themselves, in low voices, while they ate shyly, tentatively.

The one other person at the table who ate in absolute silence, and with a kind of disdain for the company at the table, was Doña Vera herself, majestically seated on what what was surely a raised chair at the head. The persona of the grande dame clearly required some contrivance.

Eric was now able to observe her at closer quarters than he had at the lecture in Mexico City: the chandelier was so positioned as to cast a particularly bright light on her while others were in shadow. She was no longer the theatrically attired diva she had chosen to be in the city, nor quite the woman who had ridden alone, calmly at ease in the light and air and space she owned. Now she was somewhere between the two extremes: dressed in a kimono in the colours of that fabulous bird, the quetzal, over layers of worn and lumpish grey flannel underneath. She might have been a carved idol placed upon her seat of power but, like an idol, she displayed the human attributes that could undercut her power: which to believe? to trust? Her nose certainly remained that of a bird of prey, an imperial beak that protruded from her sunken cheeks, but her mouth worked weakly at food that was clearly difficult for her to masticate.

She was concentrating upon that with a kind of withdrawn, inward preoccupation when, out of the general chatter – still of Huichol, peyote, Wirikúta – a question arose, addressed to her by an older member of the gathering, a small-boned, hunch-shouldered man in spectacles and a bow tie knotted over his Adam's apple, someone who could not be dismissed as easily as the youngsters. Eric had not heard the question, but he had picked out a word or two: shaman – vision – dream – trance – ecstasy . . .

The active exercise of forks and knives gradually lessened and came to a halt. In the silence, the intruding voice pursued, 'Doña Vera, can any one of us share that experience with them, do you think?'

Everyone waited, holding their implements above their plates, while Doña Vera crumbled a roll of bread and considered her reply. Then it came, as ominous as a rumble of pebbles in a dry arroyo, heard at first from a distance, then gathering strength as it approached, finally crashing upon them.

'No one,' she pronounced, 'no one who sleeps under a roof, in a bed, and eats three meals a day at a table, can understand the Huichol experience. Is that not so, maestro?' and she smiled her rare smile at the quiet man at the foot of the table. He became aware he was being addressed, fell silent and looked at her enquiringly. It was not clear if he understood her question but then he too smiled, and nodded.

Everyone else at the table was excluded from their exchange, their communication.

Fortunately the maids came out of the kitchen just then and interrupted it by serving everyone from the trayfuls of hot food they had brought. The sound of knives and forks began again, filling everyone with relief.

49

Doña Vera herself, however, rose from the table, pushing back her chair, and called to the maids to bring her coffee. Everyone paused, forks lifted in the air, waiting for the royal departure. She had taken her favourite pug with her; now the others became aware of her absence, stirred underneath the table as if they were a heap of suede gloves and velvet scarves being collected, scrambled to their feet and followed with a hasty clicking of claws on stone tiles.

Watching her leave, Eric was struck by how small she was, shrivelled and slight, for all the height she accorded herself. Also, he noticed, she had felt slippers on, and those were flannel pyjamas she was wearing under her splendid kimono. How much of it all was a costume drama, he thought, dependent on style and setting. For all that, it was still her home.

'She always takes coffee in the library,' the man with the bow tie and the rimless spectacles said to Eric, acknowledging the newcomer at last.

'The library? There is one?'

'It is my – it is where I work,' smiled a small wisp of a woman with spectacles and close-cropped hair, also daring to be friendly now.

'Ah, may I come and look at your books tomorrow?' Eric asked eagerly, scarcely able to believe his luck. 'And if you have maps, documents too, perhaps?'

'It is a great resource, a great resource,' the bow-tied man assured him, patting his lips with a napkin and making the small, short-haired woman flush with pride. 'We are just about to show a film about Doña Vera's life, in the museum. Would you care to see it? I've asked my students to attend.'

Eric wanted to point out that he was not one of them but was too polite to do so. He found himself going along with the pedagogical group, shuffling across the court-yard once more, past the fountain spouting in the dark, to the hall known as 'the museum'.

Sitting there, on an uncomfortably upright chair in a draught from the door, and waiting for the students to set up a screen and a projector, Eric castigated himself for the way he always let himself be led by autocratic people with strong opinions. Em might so far have been the strongest of them, even if the least ostensibly so, but before her there had been Rosa. The situation he was in now inevitably caused him to remember how he had been led to take courses he never would have, if it had not been for the pleasure of gazing on Rosa's head of long, glossy black hair or brushing his fingers, as if accidentally, against it. Poetry, to begin with: she wrote it and insisted he take the course with her and experience the thrill she felt from being in the presence of her teacher, a 'real poet' – an old man whose white hair had fallen out in patches, leaving only tufts, and whose lean, bony face twitched as if in pain when he listened to her read, which she thought quite appropriate since she wrote about bombings, nuclear holocausts, death by fire and the grieving of survivors. Eric attempted a few verses at her urging, but the 'real poet' himself provided none; his face twitched, his lips parted as if for air, then shut, and he kept his eyes averted as Eric did from him, out of embarrassment and apology.

Next, Rosa lured him into an even more difficult course, of feminist studies. There he found himself the sole male student. He held on through the semester even though Rosa would grill him after every class, seize his notebook to see what he had thought worth putting down on its mostly pristine pages, then throw it at him if she found no more than the occasional doodle, and challenge him to match her own fervour. Eric thought she went too far, he could not possibly follow where she wished to go but was flattered that she should want his company.

During a film they were shown in class, he finally gave up, detaching his fingers from hers. She held on as tightly as she could but it was a hot afternoon and the blinds were drawn, making the room oppressively still and stuffy – actually even smelly – and he slipped away with an apologetic murmur. When she demanded angrily later to know why he had left, he finally told her the truth: 'I couldn't stand it,' he said simply. She was furious; if it was a film by Margarethe von Trotta, she expected him to stand it. But Eric grew stubborn. He stopped taking the classes she wanted him to take or where he was likely to run into her. Eventually they met only in the cafeteria, if their schedules permitted it, and now that they had less to discuss, they made fewer appointments to meet and so became figures in the distance, crossing the campus from sunlight into the oak trees' shade, waving minimally till winter drew a curtain of snow between them.

Then, in graduate school, he met Em and once again submitted to the spell of a woman who received such certainty and confidence from her work. It perplexed him that he should be drawn to this 'type' but he was so there had to be a serious side to him in spite of their accusations of frivolity and shallowness: he hoped so. Or was it because he saw how happily, gratefully, his father submitted to work in the business his mother's family owned as if he had not really known, in the new country to which he had come, what to do with himself till she showed him? And because Eric too was used to letting his mother make up his mind for him, ordering his life, telling him what to do with it? Only, while his father appeared to be the most contented of men in his little cubbyhole of an office, keeping the accounts for 'O'Brien's', Eric did not feel he had found an equivalent niche yet. He wondered if this was what Em wanted him to find, by himself. Then, if he would find it in unravelling the intricate cat's cradle of the voyages of his own family. Were they actually relevant? Did he even believe in the pursuit?

As he sat in the dark, once more submitting to a film he did not wish to see, he felt a headache starting to clamp itself to his temples as it often did at moments of anxiety and unease.

The film was even worse than he expected. Perhaps the low voltage that was the rule in that area gave it its agonisingly slow momentum and dismal shortage of lighting. There, on the screen spotted with night insects, was the young Doña Vera riding a horse through a sepia landscape of stone and thorn while the background music ground ever downwards. Then Doña Vera posing with a group of Indians in ceremonial dress of which the colours were naturally not visible in a black-and-white film. Doña Vera interviewing a man whose face remained shaded by a conical hat and who seemed to answer her animated and long-winded questions with the merest monosyllables. Doña Vera walking across the desert in long strides, the sequence interspersed with stills of tarantulas, serpents, scorpions and other such creatures she might –

or might not – have encountered there. Doña Vera seated at a heavy, carved table, lifting up the objects on it one at a time, describing their symbolic significance.

During this sequence, the younger members of the audience began to lose patience; they started to talk to each other, quite loudly, and even laugh. The older ones in the audience concentrated with fierce attention meant to be admonitory. The music swelled to a climax which collapsed in a way that instigated involuntary laughter, and then the title unfurled across the screen in cursive script: *Queen of the Sierra* it read, with a flourish of trumpets.

One trick such experiences had taught Eric was to get to his feet quickly and make his escape before the lights came on and someone in the front row – or the last – rose 'to initiate a discussion'. That he would not have. He let himself out through the open door before he could be seen to flee.

The lights in the dining room had been turned off but there was still one on in the room to which Doña Vera had retired for coffee. In addition, there was the sound of the piano being played – very delicately, very tenderly, Eric thought. He stopped outside the window to listen and light a cigarette and found twirling up to him along with the smoke, fragrance from the white flowers of a bush of night-flowering tobacco. The music – was it a Chopin nocturne? – twirled just as delicately, seeming to accentuate the silence of the night at the foot of the mountain that loomed over the hacienda, and made it poignant and profound, even if the piano was badly out of tune so that some of the notes jarred and made the pianist falter.

Putting out his cigarette on a stone, he decided to look

in on the lighted room; he could not restrain his curiosity about the piano, how it could have been brought here to this remote altiplano, or who might be playing it – Doña Vera, perhaps?

No, it was not, he saw at once, for the Queen of the Sierra was seated by an empty fireplace in a wing chair, with her pugs. He coughed to let her know of his entrance but she made no acknowledgement unless it was in the wave of the lighted cigarillo she held.

'I thought,' he stumbled, 'I should tell you, I'm not sure how long I'll stay. I planned to do a little research but I don't know yet –'

As he might have known, the word 'research' brought her to wakefulness out of the dreamy half-sleep in which he had found her. A mocking glint appeared in her hooded eyes as she slowly turned her head to look at him.

'So, then you *are* from one of the un-i-ver-sities. Tell me which one – Tex-as? O-hi-o?' she drawled, somehow making these names sound slyly insulting.

'I'm not, no,' he was able to defend himself. 'No, it's not any formal research – yet.' Since she had not offered him a seat, he found he had to draw up a chair in order to continue. 'Really, it's just a private – quest,' he went on, then stopped to see how this word might affect her.

She drew on her cigarillo, studying him. That at least was encouraging.

'You see, my grandfather came out to Mexico to work for a mining company. He was Cornish, from a mining family and, you see, the mines in Cornwall failed. I'm not sure of the date – it would have been the early part of the century – the tens or twenties –' he felt ashamed, he knew so little – 'but definitely in this area,' he insisted, 'because I recognised the names you mentioned in your lecture in Mexico City, the one I attended, I told you I attended. That's when I heard that you run this centre for studies of this area, so I thought I'd come here to see what I could find out. I heard your family too had a connection to the mines –'

She reared out of her wing chair, a bird of prey swooping. '*Who* told you that?'

'Oh,' he drew back, alarmed; he might have been bitten, or stung. 'Oh, someone in the audience –'

'You are mis-in-formed, señor. I may be run-ning this centre and it may be fam-i-ly property, but the mines, they were before my time. I did not arrive here till the forties, and I am myself an eth-no-graph-er,' she spaced out her syllables as if for someone of lesser intelligence, 'and trained as an an-thro-polo-gist with some of the great-est teachers in the field. I have worked among the Huichol Indians, the first, the first Eu-ro-pean woman to do so. I founded my centre to pro-tect them, their en-vir-on-ment, their hist-ory, and rel-ig-ion. I am not one of those who took their land and ru-ined it with mining and made them slaves. Whoever tells you this, *lies*.' The word exploded with a clap of thunder. The little pugs shuddered in their sleep, some even gave small yips to prove their vigilance. She pressed them back to sleep with her ringed hand.

Eric, hiding his own hands between his knees, wondered if he should flee but she continued imperiously. 'If it is mines you are interested in, then it is not to me you should come. Not to my centre. Here we work to keep the cul-ture and re-lig-ion and art of the Huichol a-live that the min-ing in-dus-try near-ly de-stroy-ed. On the one hand is greed, señor, on the other – respect! Did you not see the film tonight?'

'I did, I did,' Eric hastened to assure her. 'Fascinating!' She pursed her lips, clearly expecting more.

'The work you have done here, so important,' he went on, 'so wonderful –' But why was she so defensive? If her work was as renowned and respected as she insisted, where was the need constantly to assert this?

Her lips relaxed a little. It was transparently easy to mollify the old bird, Eric saw, and went on flattering her in that vein for a bit (Em would have despised him, he knew). He wondered if he could put a question to her about the enigmatic presence of the Indians at the foot of her dinner table but just then, tapping the ash off the end of her cigarillo, she provided him with an answer as if she had sensed it. 'It is a liv-ing cult-ure, you see. I have guests in my hacienda that can prove to you its ex-is-tence. Their way of life ex-ists. That is my purpose, señor, to keep it a-live. Post-Columbian Mex-ico,' she pronounced, straightening her back, 'interests me not at all. Once those poor people were con-vert-ed by the Span-iards, it was the end, the end! And if that is the pe-riod that in-ter-ests you, señor, go up the moun-tain. *There* you will see what the mining in-dus-try did to Huichol country.'

He nodded enthusiastically to assure her he would, and she continued. 'You have come at ex-act-ly the right moment, the cel-e-bration of *el Día de los Muertos*, the Day of the Dead. Go, go and see it, please. It is right-ly named, after the dead. Here,' she tapped her cigarillo, making the ashes scatter, 'here at my centre, you find *life*! Ar-tists come to my centre, and scho-lars, and seekers.

Not his-tor-ians, and not – she fixed him with a fierce eye – 'not *mineros*!'

As he wondered how he might make his escape from further denunciation, he heard a rustle from behind the piano which was actually on the other side of the stone arch that divided the room, he now saw. Someone there, under a dim green-shaded light, was folding up the music sheets as unobtrusively as possible. The pianist rose and came forwards: it was the spectacled woman with the short grey hair who had introduced herself at dinner as the librarian. It seemed she also held the position of official musician at Doña Vera's establishment. But Doña Vera made no acknowledgement of her presence or her performance and Eric had to rise to his feet and take it upon himself to say, 'Thank you, that was just beautiful.' She gave an awkward little bow, her spectacles glinting in the subdued light, and slipped away without a word.

'Margaret,' Doña Vera suddenly bellowed after her, 'send Consuela. I go to bed now,' and at that word, as if at a bell, the heap of sleeping pugs around her stirred and scrambled to their many feet.

PART II

Vera Stays

'You are looking on rich lands. May you know how to govern them well.'

Alonso Hernandez Puertocarrero to
Hernando Cortez, 1519

Chapter 4

After the fall of the Aztec empire, the conquest of the country proceeded with wonderful rapidity, chiefly because the invaders hoped to meet with greater treasure in every mountain they beheld. The manner in which the Indian was forced to labour in the mines is well known, and how, accustomed to the gentler pursuit of agriculture, their numbers rapidly diminished.

Carl Sartorius, *Mexico and the Mexicans*, 1859

Around the immense mahogany table under the Venetian chandelier where they entertained, the gentlemen were sometimes heard to mention the Hacienda de la Soledad. Not as often as they mentioned the mines of Cinco Señores, La Joya, Guadalupe, Santa Ana, Valenciana, or the companies – Compaña Anglo-Mexicana, Bolaños, Real del Monte, Restauradora – but once in a while someone would talk of having stayed there, spent a night there on his way up or down from the mines – in their glory days. Now, Don Roderigo assured her, it was un-inhabited and uninhabitable.

Vera tired quickly of the social flutter in which she was required to participate in Mexico City. She told Don Roderigo that if that was what she had wanted from life, she could have stayed in Vienna. Of course she did not confess that she felt at a disadvantage among ladies who had lived here for so much longer than she had and were so free with advice on how to handle the maids so they would not grow slovenly or thievish, where to order a pudding or freshly baked rolls for a party or silk stockings from Paris. Nor her chagrin at their constant questioning about her past and her background and how she had come to be here among them. Her discomfort and restlessness had not the slightest effect upon her husband who simply continued with his routine of running through the family fortune at the races and the casinos, and ignored her suggestion of a visit to a place that intrigued her because of its distance from everything that made up their lives: its very name promised a refuge.

She had quickly given up being the delightfully coquettish woman he had brought back from Europe after his frail and highly bred first wife's death. She soon began to complain loudly of boredom and disappointment. 'I am not one of these silly, card-playing women of your circle,' she told him since he obviously failed to see this fact for himself. The next step was voicing her desire, at first in company and then when she was alone with him while he was digesting a gigantic meal, having his coffee and smoking his cigar, to travel outside Mexico City and see something of this land to which he had brought her.

He raised his eyelids with difficulty (she suspected something seriously wrong with them, it could not be natural for them to droop so in broad daylight even if he was twice her age). He mumbled, chewing at the idea and finding it tough.

'Can we not go on a journey?' she cried, waving her hands at him as if to attract and hold his attention. 'I have been here already a year and seen nothing, nothing at all!'

He gestured tiredly, making his cigar sweep in an aromatic circle that she found suffocating. 'Tell the chauffeur,' he mumbled, 'to take you to Teotihuacán, the pyramids . . .'

'Oh *mein Gott*, Roderigo, I have seen the pyramids of Teotihuacán, how many times! Taken all our visitors there, don't you know that? I am as good as a paid guide already to the pyramids of Teotihuacán. Has Mexico nothing more to offer?'

He began to look annoyed. He chewed on his cigar. He did not trouble to raise his eyelids. 'Xochimilco, then,' he offered, 'the floating gardens . . .'

'The floating gardens!' she shrieked. 'What next?'

Then he did lift those lids to give her a withering glare: she was growing shrill, this blonde butterfly of a woman, his European trophy – 'the fresh rosebud in his lapel,' someone had called her – whom he had met on his last European tour undertaken, disastrously, just before the outbreak of World War II. The family had despatched him to get in touch with former business partners: the price of precious metals had risen, other mines were being revived – why not theirs? But, although Roderigo knew the racecourses and clubs of Europe, he knew little else and understood nothing. Bewildered by the way his former business partners seemed suddenly to be distracted or even to have gone underground, he had little to do but search for distraction himself. Then the attractive blonde girl he had spotted earlier on the arm of one of those uniformed and bemedalled military men who were suddenly ubiquitous, and again on the stage as a dancer in the chorus of a lively musical show in a theatre he had wandered into, reappeared in the lobby of his hotel. When he went into the dining room for his daily consolation of *Wiener schnitzel* and *Apfelstrudel*, there she was again, alone at a table, casting him flirtatious looks. Flattered, charmed, he responded with all the gallantry he could summon.

When it finally dawned upon him that no business was to be done that summer in Austria, or in Germany, and he regretfully informed her that he had to return to Mexico, she conveyed such an all-consuming interest in his home and family and business in that faraway land, their sugarcane estates, their timber holdings, and the property they owned in Mexico City and the 'Silver Cities' of the north, such a curiosity and enthusiasm, that he even began to consider her as a replacement for the dear departed Doña Josefina. The speed with which she agreed to be his wife and with which she packed and prepared to leave did fluster him: it was not the way he was used to acting himself, even if he could see that circumstances had changed and called for changed behaviour. It was she who searched for berths on an earlier boat than he had managed to find, insisting that they travel to England and catch one from Liverpool that would take them to New York and from there to Vera Cruz. Dismayed, he asked if this was really necessary, upon which she became nearly hysterical, demanding if he did not *understand*. Of course he did, he assured her, but clearly did not since he asked if she did not wish to spend some time with her family before she left. She assured him she had none. No family? That did give him pause, but before he could enquire further, they were boarding the boat for New York. During the entire voyage she was prostrate with seasickness and nerves and unable to come out on deck or into the dining room to meet other passengers. 'It might do you good,' he tried to persuade her. 'You would enjoy the company of a charming Herr Levi I have met. Or of Herr Wolfowitz and his wife . . .' She practically fainted then, begging him not to speak to them of his poor, sick bride.

He remembered that now, as he regarded this shrill, shrieking woman whose cheeks were no longer porcelain white but red as a cook's with anger, her blonde curls damp on her forehead. No longer attractively dressed in pale blue or pink tulle or crêpe de Chine but still in her nightdress and slippers, and without cosmetics or perfume. Doña Josefina would never have appeared thus at table, he reflected, never. She continued to complain – of boredom, of uneducated company: 'merchants, shop-keepers, ranchers! And once I dined with generals, colonels, directors!' – till he heaved himself to his feet, shouting, 'And why were you so eager to leave them, their company, your glorious country, and come here?' She stopped her harangue then and looked at him, appalled. 'Because it was all destroyed,' she said at last, in a much lower, less confident voice. 'You didn't see it but I did – how it was all up, finished.' 'So then you are lucky, are you not,' he demanded, 'to have come away?' and lurched off himself, to his study and the soothing company of his Great Dane, El Duque, and the silver flask of brandy behind the leather-bound volumes of the encyclopaedia. He sat in his great leather chair and El Duque laid a drooling jowl upon his slippered foot with a groan of sympathy. Fondling the dog's ears, he grumbled at himself under his breath for not having made enquiries about the woman he was to marry and her mysterious lack of family or means.

He ought to have paid more attention. Even now, with Roderigo long since dead and buried in the family vault where no one visited him, it gave her satisfaction to think how mistaken he had been and how much he must have regretted it when, leaving him to a family council in San Luis Potosí to which he had insisted she come, she had slipped away, scandalously alone, and visited for herself the Hacienda de la Soledad, the house at the foot of the mountain from which the silver had been extracted that made the family wealthy, wealthy enough to own this hacienda among so many others. The others, however, being occupied by his mother, his aunts, his sisters and brothers-in-law, nieces and nephews, uncles and cousins, had been so many extensions of the prison house in 'the best locality' in Mexico City to which he had brought her, while the Hacienda de la Soledad was from the very first her own: no one else wanted it.

In all her European years, she had never had solitude or space. No one in Roderigo's family or circle could know how she had lived – the small, cramped apartment at the top of a building of stained and peeling stucco, its dripping walls, torn linoleum and its battered stove and pots, smells of lavatories down the hall and cabbage cooking in the kitchen, and the fear of losing even that.

She had made her way out of it, first by catching the eye of one of the men newly arrived in their city who dined nightly in a restaurant at a table on which she waited, then by persuading him to pay for dancing lessons, something her own parents could not afford to give her. This had led to small roles in musical shows put on in theatres scattered across the city, but she had made the most of them, she had not gone unnoticed. There had been rewards – bouquets sent around to the stage door, invitations to parties, the occasional weekend in a country villa. Of course there was the unavoidable return to the family, its querulous needs and demands and criticism, but these ceased mercifully once she was able to find positions through her new friends and patrons for her father and brothers – lowly ones, true, but in these difficult times even those were welcome. If they did not last, she was not to blame (although her mother clearly did: 'I told you so,' she shrieked the night Vera's father came home bloody and beaten by a group of anti-Nazis, 'I told you so!') Next it was the director at the theatre, polite and circumspect Herr Schmidt with his spotless white cuffs and cashmere cravat, beckoning her into his office as she went by in her costume and make-up and perspiring from her dance, to warn her to be careful of her friends 'because we cannot protect you out there'. Coming from him, the words had authority. She had not been unaware of the rumours and fears swirling thick and dark around them, making everyone realise that the bright lights were about to go out, only she had so much wanted it all to last.

It was then, in the hotel where she went to see if one familiar face could be found to reassure her of the protection she had enjoyed, that Roderigo appeared instead – large, foolish and fumbling, but all fresh linen, gleaming leather and the smell of bay rum. An outsider, a foreigner, presenting an opening to a foreign world. Not that she had ever craved one before, or had any idea of what it might be – the places and people he named were unknown to her – but compelling for precisely that reason.

A graveyard of history – that was what she found herself surveying when she first saw the Hacienda de la Soledad, a ruin of blackened stones, fallen beams and cavernous halls where her footsteps sounded like hammers tapping on the great stone tiles. All around parched land with the wind roaring like an unimpeded flood through its emptiness. She had herself driven up the mountain and followed streets silenced by white dust and lined with doorless, windowless and often roofless houses in which lizards hid among weeds. On the steps of the cathedral, so immense and so grand as to seem like a mirage in the blinding light, some Franciscan priests wrapped in shadowy robes watched her pass. She asked the chauffeur to continue along a dirt track where a few adobe walls stood among the thorn trees and cacti up to the scarred and flattened mountain top. Here she ordered him to stop outside the whitewashed walls around a silent cemetery and its desolate chapel on a rock, and got out to walk. He came out after her with her linen hat and she put it on irritatedly, and waved him away, then set out to find some trace of the mines that had once belonged to Roderigo. Except for a few abandoned excavations and ruined entrances to shafts and tunnels, there was none. The silence was so intense that she could hear the wings of the zopilotes circling watchfully above on currents of air; she had to imagine the sounds the mountain must once have contained – explosions of dynamite, small avalanches of gravel followed by the thunder of falling boulders, the rumble of metal trolleys along rusty tracks, jackhammers, whistles and sirens. She felt certain their echoes must still resound and, seeing the dark eye of a cave in the mountainside, entered it in the desire to hear that pounding and beating for herself. Perhaps even the hooves of Zapata's horses, carrying the message of the Revolution: '*¡Tierra y Libertad!*' Taking a few steps into that darkness, she was brought to a standstill by the total absence of light. Not a chink, not a shaft, and not the possibility of one: it could only grow darker, blacker, more totally. Still, she stood waiting to see if something would materialise – an eye that watched, a movement.

There was a scramble of footsteps on the gravel, the panting breath of someone quite distraught. 'Señora, señora,' the chauffeur called, 'come back, instantly, I beg you.' When she did, she found him whey-faced and listened to his scolding. 'There are rattlesnakes there, scorpions as big as your hand. Shafts you could fall through. Please, please, what would the señor say to me?'

She gave him a disdainful smile and had him drive her back to the hacienda, telling him to go and find the caretaker while she took another look around. She went down to a jacaranda tree on the slope below from where she could look out over a shallow lake on fire with afternoon light, and the mesa beyond, taking on the purple and crimson brushstrokes of evening. '*Tierra y Libertad*,' she said to herself and then, realising there was no one to hear, shouted out, '*¡Tierra y Libertad!*'

The chauffeur, sitting on a bench outside the caretaker's hut with the mug of *café con leche* he had been given, muttered to himself that he had always suspected she was *una loca*.

Once she had moved in, Vera engaged the man who acted as caretaker of the hacienda, and lived below it in a shed enclosed by a fence of cacti and thorn, to lend her one of the horses he kept among the more useful burros, pigs and turkeys, and teach her to ride it. The first time she mounted it and set off, she said to herself that this was how she would make the land hers.

She knew she would have to be strong to live here:

she had to kill scorpions daily in the ruins of the house before it was repaired, and sometimes the silence was so intense that she could hear the termites' tiny jaws gnawing at the beams above her while sawdust rained down on the furniture, the floor, her bed, her hair. Once, on a hot, still night, she left the windows of her room unshuttered as she fell asleep and in the night was awakened by a searing pain on her shoulder. There was no one to call for help till morning when the caretaker's wife came, looked at the blister growing there, and told her it was surely caused by the urine of a bat. Vera remembered that some had swooped in and around at dusk, and screamed at the woman for help. She did eventually bring it – there was no doctor or hospital for miles – in the form of an old sorceress and Vera had had to submit to her potions and poultices which, it had to be admitted, did bring down the swelling, although the scar never vanished.

On another occasion, a half-starved man appeared in the courtyard long after the door to the road had been locked for the night. She sent him around to the kitchen for bread and told her reluctant maids to let him stay the night on sacks in the storeroom where supplies of maize, rice, beans, sugar, coffee and tobacco were kept. As they predicted, he was gone by morning, along with silver candlesticks from the table and the ornate gilt clock she had brought from Mexico City. The caretaker came that afternoon to inform her that the police were enquiring after a man who had escaped from prison where he was held on a charge of murder. 'Still, he was a beggar,' she said to Jaime, 'should he have been sent away hungry?' and she said nothing to Roderigo when he came on one of his rare visits.

Every day she made herself ride miles out alone and learn how to endure the sun and thirst and solitude. She rode over the mesa where a stranger could easily be lost in the featureless monotony of rubble and learned that it had secret features and contours for those who looked. There were invisible arroyos marked only by an unexpected stand of drooping alamos or *ahuehueté* trees, and an occasional isolated rancho with flat-topped adobe huts where dogs barked to see her pass and women stopped pounding maize or scrubbing laundry in shallow troughs to gaze at her in silence. These ranchos would be fringed with dry corn stalks that seemed to mutter and murmur to each other conspiratorially, in a language she had to master.

The sun followed her through the day, a fierce and watchful eye. She found the evenings best, when the sky paled, the earth darkened and the air lost its harshness and turned gentler, mild. Occasionally she stayed out so late that she would decide to camp for the night instead of returning home; and she would light a small fire of brush in the lee of some boulders and lie rolled in a blanket to listen to her horse pawing at the stones and watch the stars wheel overhead.

It was there that she had her first encounter with the Huichol. Winding uphill in single file like pilgrims from an earlier, primal world, some barefoot, some in soundless sandals, they had bows and arrows with them and carried bags slung over their shoulders, clearly still hunter-gatherers. Although they politely returned her greeting, they did not pause or show the slightest interest in her foreign presence: she might have been a cactus to get around or a stone they had stumbled upon. She could not make out who they might be: she could see from their dress and appearance that they were not local people who were all farmers or herders. On returning to the hacienda, she asked Jaime, when he came to help her dismount, if he knew. 'Huichol, Huichol,' he told her. It was the first time that she heard the word. He went on to tell her that it was the time of year when they came on their long pilgrimage from as far away as Nayarit and Jalisco in search of the peyote cactus that grew only in this region. He described it to her but she could never see it, it blended in so completely with the pebbly rubble of the soil. Why would they want it so much as to come some three hundred miles on foot to collect it? she wondered, and Jaime, laughing, told her how it gave them visions that made them see the spirits they worshipped. 'So they're not *catalicos*?' she asked. 'No, no,' Jaime assured her, and called them, derisively, '*paganos*', heathens.

Vera, who despised Jaime and his slatternly wife and their numerous snuffling children and thought of them, privately, as half-caste, found her curiosity aroused by the aloofness and self-containment of the Huichol she had seen, characterisitics, she thought, of a higher level of being, but she was cautious. She knew she would have to be patient and wait, not make any hasty or overt attempt to engage them till they became used to her following them on their route, at a discreet distance, and came to see her as unthreatening. (Jaime had told her they were afraid of running into local farmers or ranchers who would chase them off their property and have them arrested for trespassing.) So it was a long time before she even attempted to convey to them, through gestures and a little Spanish, on finding a group so fatigued and dehydrated that thcy had sunk on to their haunches in the midday blaze of heat and seemed hardly able to proceed, that her hacienda was open to them and they could come in and refresh themselves. She had tables set out in the court-yard, and pitchers of water and *té de Jamaica* brought out to them by her supercilious maids who expressed resentment at having to serve them till she was able to teach them better. She had her visitors show her their embroidery and beadwork and the decorated pots they had brought with them, and bought pieces to display on the walls and tables of her huge, echoing rooms. When Roderigo came and brought an occasional visitor, it was clear they thought her crazy to collect such objects but when she insisted on their taking some back to the city for display and sale, they were equally amazed to discover that folk art had become fashionable (thanks to such flamboyant leaders of the art world as Frida Kahlo and Diego Rivera), and could actually be sold. Vera saw to it that the Huichol received the profits. Their gratitude gave her an inkling of what it might be not to be the recipient but the distributor of largesse.

A letter arrived enquiring about her growing collection. It bore a stamp and a name that were recognisably Germanic, and made her heart clench as if it were locking itself up. She did not reply. But the author of the letter – which had the letterhead of the Museum für Völkerkunde in Berlin-Dahlem – did not give up and enlisted other Meso-Americanists to plead with her to share what she knew of Huichol lore and legend, artefacts and objects.

At that time, she knew nothing and how could she confess that? She wanted nothing to do with academics who would only expose her ignorance: she had no book learning to speak of. What was she to tell them – that she had learned to act and dance instead?

So she held out till it dawned upon her that her position was a unique one and she could make something of that. Something that would either impress or appal Roderigo and his family – probably the latter. At the end of a particularly long, arid day when Jaime and his family and the kitchen staff were all away at a fiesta, the silence rang in her ears as if she were the only living person on earth, and she relented and agreed to a visit by a pair of scholars, from the Instituto Nacional Indigenista. It was a very long way for them to come but, once there, they were sufficiently impressed to declare it the perfect setting for a conference of Meso-Americanists. That was when her defences truly collapsed. She whirled around – and made her resistant staff whirl too – to have the hacienda polished, buffed, furbished and refurbished to receive her guests. In a panic, she even begged friends in Mexico City (never considered 'friends' before) to send help – and they sent her Maggie Paget, a young English girl in need (an orphan serving as a companion to her godmother in Yucatán, she had been left stranded by the old lady's death), who brought with her, in a cart filled with hay, a Bosendorfer piano, and from the first day made herself indispensable. The conference was a success – and the legend of Doña Vera was launched.

The younger of the academics had even stayed on to make a film about her life. Being the star of a film – how could she have resisted that? It had seemed as if, in the most bizarre and unexpected way, her past had found a way to fuse with the present. Posing for them on horseback amid the cacti or in her courtyard with her arms around her Huichol friends, she flashed a smile at the camera such as she had always been meant to but never had before.

Perhaps if she had known then what it would all lead to, she would never have begun. If she had known, she would not have shared her Huichol with anyone, but joined them in the mountains, alone. As it was, she now had pathetic creatures like the young man she had just dismissed come and sit at her table, waiting for some crumbs to fall. There they sat, worrying – she could see how they worried – about their research papers, their dissertations, their careers, their little pining lives. Coming out to the Sierra in the hope that she, and of course the Huichol, would open doors to vaster, richer worlds. They reminded her of the *mineros* searching in desperation for less and less productive veins of gold, or the missionaries who infiltrated everywhere in search of souls to collect for the Lord. Now these souls had to be collected for another instituition, the university. Doña Vera despised all equally.

She remembered one silly woman she had had as a guest, a very silly woman indeed who clasped her hands to her bosom and exclaimed, with shining eyes, 'Oh, I wish I had been born a Huichol woman! Perhaps in my next life I will be born one!' to which she had snapped – quite aware that she had had such moments and aspirations herself once – 'Yes? You think you will be able to grind corn and light the fire and make tortillas for your men while they are sleeping off a night's drinking? And have a new baby every year tied in your *rebozo* to nurse?' and the woman had cringed.

Many years later it still pleased her to think of putting

that woman in her place. Not up in the clouds but down, at her feet. You had to have lived in Europe in the times when she did, to have survived and succeeded where people around you were falling to pieces, starving, going off to prison – or somewhere – never to be heard from again, to know what it took.

The old irritation and scorn returned. She called after Consuela, half asleep on her feet as she carried away the coffee tray, 'Have you cleared the dining table? Have you set it for breakfast? Have you remembered the fresh napkins?' and she waited, her hand on the banister, to see Consuela put out the lights, one by one, leaving just the one on the staircase for her to go up to her own apartment, leaving the house below in darkness so that the crickets could come out and begin to chirp and the owl in the tree outside to call: they knew their roles in her house.

Eric, left in semi-darkness, could not resist peering into the library where a light was still on. He both surprised and was himself surprised by Miss Paget who had not retired but appeared to be still at work behind a pile of books at her desk. 'I didn't mean to startle you,' Eric at once said on seeing her put her hand to her mouth in alarm. 'I – um – I just hoped to pick up something to read in bed. But –'

She rose at once, smoothing down her collar and straightening her spectacles. (Eric could not help wondering if she had been having a drink behind her books.) 'Can I help?' she offered, as if it were ten in the morning, the library open and she on duty.

Eric wandered around, stroking desktops and book spines as if reacquainting himself with a familiar world which, in a way, he was. 'Um – a history, perhaps? Is there one of the mining town above? It's what I've come to see.'

Miss Paget pondered, then shook her head. But she did find him two books she thought provided information on 'modern' Mexico. 'Most of what we have here is on pre-Columbian Mexico,' she explained, and handed him Alexander von Humboldt's *Political Essay on the Kingdom of New Spain* and Carl Sartorius's *Mexico and the Mexicans*. 'But these are nineteenth century,' she said, 'so there's sure to be much on the mining industry.'

'Just the thing,' he assured her, and thanked her profusely before he left. From the weight of the books, their dustiness and the dates they bore – 1811 and 1859 – he was certain they would help to put him to sleep.

Professor Wainwright, lowering himself on to his bed, bent to unlace his shoes. Mrs Wainwright studied him over the top of her book. She could not keep a somewhat smug expression from her greasily lotioned and rose-scented face: she had slipped away before she could be made to see *Queen of the Sierra* yet again, and spent a happy hour in bed with a thriller instead. 'So, what did the students think of it?' she asked because she could not refrain from rubbing it in, her little triumph.

The professor removed his glasses and put them carefully away. 'I did not ask,' he replied after a moment. 'I did not want to hear.'

She chortled. '*And* she got in that line about not understanding anything unless you sleep on stones and freeze.'

'Well, yes,' he agreed, sliding a finger under his bow tie to loosen it. 'She always does.'

'I guess it was for the benefit of the new guy,' said his

wife, the thriller having made her wide awake and alert. 'Couldn't be for *us*, we've heard it too often.'

He rose to his feet and stretched, snapping his braces and yawning.

'One year,' she said, and she too had said it before, 'just *one* year, we should go to Acapulco instead,' and turned back to the thriller.

Eric, returning to his room and feeling a wave of tiredness take him up and roll him over, was undressing listlessly when he became aware that the room was unusually warm and stuffy: a fire was burning in the grate. It irritated him somehow unendurably: why, on a warm night, should anyone light a fire? And who was it that so freely used the poor, diminished resources of this land in order to provide it to foreign tourists, even if unasked for and unwanted? What would *Em* think? And what, too, would she say about it to Doña Vera?

He threw open the window to let out the smoke, lowered himself on to the bed and let the cool night air enter and wash over him. He soon found that it had the effect of making him wide awake again. Although his bones were aching from the journey, his head was suddenly clear. He picked up the *Political Essay* and read:

The Indian tenateros, *the beasts of burden in the mines of Mexico, remain loaded with a weight of 275 to 300 pounds for a span of six hours. In the galleries of Valenciana, they are exposed to temperatures of 22° to 25° (71–75°F) and during this time they ascend and descend several thousands of steps in pits of an inclination of 45°. The* tenateros *carry the minerals in bags made of the threads of* pité. *To protect their shoulders (for the mineros are generally naked to the middle) they place a woolen covering under this bag. We meet in the mine some 50 or 60 of these porters, among whom are men above sixty and boys of ten or twelve years of age. In ascending the stairs they throw their bodies forwards and rest on a staff. They walk in a zigzag direction because they have found from long experience that their respiration is less impeded when they traverse obliquely the current of air which enters the pits from without.*

At this point he laid the book across his chest to face, unimpeded, that same current of air as had met the miners, forcing them to adopt the lurching, zigzag motion that he felt he had been, throughout his journey, imitating. Was this the world his grandfather had found when he crossed the ocean and sought out new territory where he might stake his claim? The effort to enter that past, as if it were a mine that no light pierced and where no air circulated, exhausted Eric and he gave himself up to sleep, gratefully.

In the library, Miss Paget turned off the last of the green-shaded lamps, having first made her desktop clear and tidy for the morning. She knew Doña Vera did not like the lights kept on after she had retired. In fact, one of her duties was to walk down the length of the corridor and make sure the resident students had switched off their lights, too. This Doña Vera had instructed her to do but, although she did walk down the corridor on her way to her small room at the end of it, she could not bring herself to tap on anyone's door and call out. There were things that Maggie Paget would not do, not even for Doña Vera. She comforted herself by saying softly, 'Shh, shh,' outside the doors where she heard voices, and laughter, and by the thought that they would not hear her. Silence and invisibility were *her* life's lessons.

In her room, Doña Vera removed her kimono, dropping it where Consuela would pick it up in the morning. It was shot silk in the colours of the quetzal, and when it fell away, she was reduced to an inner layer of grey cotton so that a reverse cycle had been performed from that of chrysalis to butterfly or fledgling to peacock. In that drab garb, she went across to the painted armoire. It creaked as she opened it so that she could look at the leather-framed photograph on the shelf of Ramón, the first, dear, dearest, dearest of all Huichol friends she had made – oldest, dearest, most beloved. Here he was, Ramón, when young, dressed in snow-white cotton, a wide belt of embroidery and a straw hat from which small emblems of the peyote cactus dangled like six- or eight- or twelve-petalled flowers. He was smiling; she too smiled, and they were young together, younger. Soon it would be *el Día de los Muertos*, and she touched his face in the photograph – black blending with sepia – and said, 'Ramón,' her lips parting with the crackling sound of paper being torn. 'Ramón, if I put out tequila for you tomorrow, and a cigar, and tamales, then, will you come? Will you?' But the face in the photograph looked past her, smiling, while she caressed the feather-tipped arrows he had given her, and felt the feathers caress her in return. She tried to make him meet her eyes but she had taken the photograph in slanting light, he had trouble looking directly at her, he squinted and looked into the distance, smiling as if he did not hear her. She had asked him year after year and he had not come – the tequila was left untouched, the cigar unlit, the tamales uneaten.

She hurled the door to the armoire shut, almost splitting it, causing her pugs to yelp with alarm, and went over to her bed and lay down, crossing her arms on her breast and closing her eyes on the luminous image of him.

He had been brought to her as a boy who had hurt his arm while on the pilgrimage, the youngest member of a group from Nayarit. They had all been weakened by that long journey, and the fasting that went with it, and the trek over the stony terrain. She had ordered the kitchen staff to provide them with food straight away and invited them to stay. They refused but when she saw they had a young boy with them who held his arm in such agony and yet held back his tears, she brought out her box of medicines and bandages, and treated it.

Any other child would have winced and cried. Instead, he kept his eyes wide open, gazing around him as if the objects he saw compensated him for his pain. At the end of the painful procedure, he ran across to what had clearly captivated him – the pug that a Franciscan father had presented to her on a visit just that afternoon, so small and so bizarre with its dark frown drawn down over its head like a stocking mask. Lifting it on to his lap, he had cradled the dog and made its little curl of a tail wag for the first time since it had entered her house. Watching, she felt certain that this was the place for the child to be – in her home, with her. Yet, when the family left and he with them, she was struck by the fear that she and her little pug would not see the boy again, he would surely die on the way. They promised to stop next year and, when they did not, she was certain he *had* died.

He reappeared three years later, grown into a youth, agile and fit, springing down the mountain from rock to rock to greet her. He was cured – he showed her the scar on his arm, healed and pink and silken to touch – and he was older, aware – as not before – of his beauty and charm. Unlike his family who had been made nervous by her house and all that she owned and offered them, he was eager to see it again and accept what she had to give. Where was Bandido? he asked, remembering the pug dog's name. It was the beginning of a legendary friendship, irregular and infrequent but revived over some ten years, again and again – till, abruptly, it ended.

Now, supine, she felt that loss again, the black coyote that hunted her down at night. She nearly broke out again into the howl she had uttered on hearing of his death – senseless, pointless, falling from a roof he was repairing in his village (so his family said, while others maintained it was in pursuit of a girl who lived nearby, and still others that it was when he was being chased by someone with a knife after a drunken brawl and that he had taken too much peyote and run out of control, but what did it matter what they said?) – throwing open her arms to catch him when he fell. She had promised to take care of him – why had she not?

If she did howl out loud, no one heard – or, if they did, they would have taken it for a dog baying on a rancho in the dark, or even a coyote on the mountainside.

If they had looked out of their windows, they would have seen the heaving mass of the tree outside, and the outline of the mountain against the night sky, interrupting those profound depths pierced by stars.

The armoire creaked open, waking her, and in the dark, Ramón the god appeared, no longer flesh and blood but paint and mask and feathers, a wooden idol whose eyelids moved. They lifted, and the eyes that looked out were real and alive. They stared at her, lying on her bed, old and ugly and shrunken – because she too was real and alive. His wooden lips parted to smile but, instead of smiling, they uttered a caw. The lips were beaks, painted beaks that cawed. It was not Ramón but a *zopilote* pretending to be Ramón, and it was leading an army of *zopilotes* that was emerging from the armoire, two by two, in perfect formation. They were not flying but walking, marching, kicking out their big clawed feet and stiff booted legs that might have looked wooden if they had not also looked military.

It would be best not to be there when they arrived. She rolled over in bed and tried to crawl out of the room unnoticed but found every exit blocked, crowded now with people. She pushed at them and screamed at them to let her pass. They turned faces to her that were bird masks, with beaks shut and eyes closed, and they pushed back, pushing her further and further into the centre of the room where a cage stood in place of her bed. She realised they were trying to put her into it, but she could not let them. She fought them as best she could, and the closer she was pressed towards the cage, the more fiercely she fought. Only they were so very many, and their hands were merging into one solid bank of hands that were made of stone. The stones were being set up all around her. If she would not get into the cage, they would enclose her within stone walls instead because the truth was this was no magical mountain-top refuge: she had tricked herself into it and was a prisoner here, there was no escape. She was being slowly suffocated to death – screaming, struggling and suffocating. Her hands tore at the stones, and she panted – let me breathe, let me breathe, let me breathe – while heaving for breath.

After such a night, morning could only come as a relief. Not disappointment at finding herself where she was, this place in which she had confined herself, but relief at being here, nowhere else, and that she was flooded by the daylight of everyday. She had never imagined that one day that would be all she wanted of life. Perhaps age made it seem almost sufficient.

Almost, not quite: that would not have been Doña Vera's way. Easing herself out of bed, she went in slippers to the window to feel the sun that blazed on her with such force. Her eye fell, unluckily, on the figure of her new guest seated beneath the jacaranda tree, turning over the leaves of a book. No doubt a book from her library. Annoyed at seeing him, she muttered to herself as she washed and dressed: Have you nothing better to do but sit in my garden and amuse yourself with my books? Do you think my role is to be your provider?

When she went down, she shouted through the kitchen door for coffee and rolls to be brought, then gave orders for all the silver to be polished. 'Today?' asked the maid, dismayed. It was *el Día de los Muertos* and she had planned to go with the groom to the *panteón* –

'Today! Now!'

Unaware that he had been observed, Eric sat under the feathery tree and read Carl Sartorius on the Indians who worked the mines:

Frequently they have to ascend a thousand or fifteen hundred feet, not by ladders but by means of the trunks of trees in which steps have been hewn. As tallow candles only are allowed in mines, the workman must shelter his light with one hand, so that the draught may not extinguish it, and have therefore only a slight hold on the other. He thus moves upward with his burthen, the trunk being slightly inclined, and secured by props every fifteen feet, the abyss on either side, into which a false step precipitates him. Indians have been known to carry up from five hundredweight in this manner, in leather sacks.

Looking up at the mountains that stood in the pure light of the milk-blue sky as if they had never been trod upon by man or beast, Eric failed to relate them to such toil. Nor could he see where his grandfather stood in relation to them, that small neat man in the brown cardigan with the leather patches who had shown him a toy train. Surely he could not have laboured as the Indians did. Nor had he possessed any share of the mines, although he must have profited. How much of what had driven him to come here was sheer necessity and how much adventure? His motives and his role were to Eric an anomaly, a disturbing one. Placing a finger between the leaves of the book to mark his page, he turned instead to watching the flight of white birds appearing from nowhere and sailing down through the gauzy air to the glistening lake below.

In the library, Miss Paget, red-faced, was confronting Doña Vera about lending books to an overnight visitor. He had asked for a book on the mining history of the town, she explained, and since they had none, she had found him von Humboldt's *Essay* and Carl Sartorius's account. Was that not right?

Doña Vera was too angry to speak for a while. When she did, she sputtered, 'A book on mining, did you say? What? What? We are not a mu-se-um of min-er-alogy here, are we? Did you tell him he has made a miss-take? I will tell him so –'

Miss Paget was both frightened and remorseful. They had had such visitors before, innocent tourists who imagined this was some inn where they could pause before climbing the mountain to the fabled ghost town above, unaware of what Doña Vera had created here, this centre of research and showplace of Huichol art. This young man had seemed a more serious tourist, but she had been mistaken, and Doña Vera had found her out. So early in the morning . . .

The students who sat at the long tables looking through books (and writing postcards home) watched and listened as discreetly as possible, but on hearing Doña Vera's opinion of the visitor, could not help small smiles and glances at each other (there was not much other entertainment after all).

Then they lifted their heads and watched as she marched out of the library into the garden beyond and called loudly for the gardener so she could give him a dressing down too. So, this was to be one of those days at the Hacienda de la Soledad, was it?

But when they assembled for lunch, with Doña Vera presiding over the great tureen of soup and seeing to it that the basket of rolls was passed up and down the length of the table, her mood had changed again. No one could know this but it was as if the last black, bitter shreds of

the night had finally receded; she had driven them out –
with her temper, and her authority – and now they
cowered in a corner, presumably rallying themselves for
their next assault but at least for the time being, for the
day, the triumph was hers.

Also, she appeared to want to put on something of a
display – not for this usual lot of visitors, students from
some university or the other, she did not even remember which one – but for the new guest who was not sufficiently apprised, evidently, of her work. This she could
not tolerate. She demanded respect from him, from
everybody; no one could leave her presence without her
having wrested that. So, over the soup, she gave one of
the talks of which they had heard, they were so legendary,
but that she seldom delivered nowadays. She spoke like
one inspired, of the Huichol trinity of peyote, deer and
maize, of the wolf shaman and the rites he undergoes
to get in touch with his animal spirit and become a wolf
with a wolf's knowledge of the world, and of the hunting
of the deer on foot, the sacrifice accompanied by the
imbibing of peyote, the Huichol knowledge of plants,
their pharmacology of plants and their uses in the treat-
ment of diseases and ailments, and how they had discovered inoculation against the dreaded smallpox long
before any European had dared make the experiment –
'Am I right, Professor Wainwright?' she called across
the table.

He knew better than to be drawn in, and letting his
soup spoon pause in its regular passage between mouth
and bowl, he smiled and nodded and refrained from
speaking.

Eric too held his tongue and did not enter into any

discussion that might expose his ignorance and call for further instruction.

She threw him a sharp look every now and then to see if she was making an impression on him. 'So then,' she wound up, 'we do what we can to pre-serve their way of life, the sa-cred way, and not de-stroy it. Who wants to see de-struc-tion may go –' she pointed a finger in the air – 'up the mountain,' and flung a triumphant look around the table. When the students burst into sponta-neous applause, she looked as gratified as a cat and fingered the heavy pendant dangling on her chest.

Out in the courtyard, the señora's three Huichol guests – two cousins and a nephew of Ramón's – sat in the shade of the corridor with their handicrafts displayed on a table. Day after day they spread them out although there were few customers apart from the occasional batch of these students, on summer internships, who came and bought the cheapest souvenirs to take home, and practised on them what little they had picked up of the Huichol language.

So they kept themselves occupied with making more and more of the bead wristlets and the yarn paintings of the deer hunt and peyote, hoping Doña Vera would take another carload to be sold in the city or, even better, take them with her to the city one day.

It was hot at midday. Little doves ran about on their curled pink toes in the blue shade of the jacaranda tree, searching among the fallen twigs and scattered leaves as if they had mislaid something. Their wings were speck-led as eggs and they blended in so well with the pebbles that they would not have been visible had it not been for their movement, constant and hurried, or their voices, conversing among themselves in soothing undertones.

'Look,' one of the craftsmen said drowsily, brushing aside the straw emblems that dangled from his hat, 'a car comes.'

The other two looked up in hope, following the banner of dust as it unfurled along the dirt road rounding the lake. Then, 'It is only the priest,' another said in disgust, 'he *never* buys,' and they returned to their beads and yarn and beeswax.

The maids too had seen the car approach from the kitchen window as they washed up. They wiped their hands and hurried to let in Fray Junípero, nearly as dusty and decrepit as the car, in his rusty old cassock that smelt of all the years of service it had given him. But they bent their knees and crossed their aproned chests dutifully, and escorted him into Doña Vera's room off the library.

She took her time before appearing: Fray Junípero was one of the afflictions that she put up with and she did so with scant grace. She did call for coffee, however, and did not have to tell them it was to be accompanied by brandy and cigars.

'You look as if you have been batt-ling the pagans again, Father,' she said to him drily, filling both a cup and a glass for him. 'Have Christ's forces still not tri-umphed?'

'The battle is perpetual, daughter,' Fray Junípero replied, mopping his face with a handkerchief as large as a kitchen towel before he drank down the tiny cup of coffee and turned gratefully to the goblet of brandy. 'No sooner is my back turned than they bring in their little pieces of string and wax and claws and feathers and Heaven alone knows what else in their bundles to offer to our blessed Virgin.'

'And does she accept?'

'She accepts all, in her grace and generosity,' he admitted. 'It is left to me to chastise and to teach. You may bring candles and light them, and flowers, I tell them – and they do, bless them, in armfuls, in mountains, even if they go without shoes – but bring in none of your objects of black magic, I beg, remove them if you do not wish to be punished.'

'And do they?'

'Ah, daughter, do they? You know as well as I do their little tricks,' he sighed, and took a sip of brandy for consolation. 'When my back is turned, they will even bring in a chicken or a rooster or a bottle of tequila as an offering. Then I have to sweep them out of the Lord's sacred home, these pagan offerings.'

'Give up, Father,' she told him, 'give up, and let the old gods back. It is their land, you know.'

He looked at her with mild reproach in his little faded eyes, not really allowing her mockery to distract him from the pleasures of her fine brandy. Thanks be to Don Roderigo for his cellar and to the *soldados* for sparing it in their wars. 'You do not really mean that, I know,' he murmured, forgiving her.

She leaned forward in her chair, holding on to its arms so that she nearly doubled over her pet pug who gave a squeal of protest. 'And you know that I do, I do. They are my gods too – I acc-ept-ed them when I came here, and they are more po-wer-ful than yours, you know.'

He wagged his finger at her, reprimanding. 'You are teasing, daughter, as you always do. But it is not a joke. Let us not joke about matters of such seriousness.'

'Ah, Father, you know as well as I do that they bring these of-fer-ings to the Virgen Maria because to them she is not that, she is their own goddess To-nant-zin, and *that* is why they bring her the vo-tive of-fer-ings that *she* prefers.'

Now he was genuinely shocked and offended. Drawing his rusty skirts about him, he spoke as sternly as the brandy permitted him. 'No, no, no,' he said so sharply, in stac-cato, that the pugs rose to their feet out of their sleep stupor and uttered shrill yips, sensing danger. 'That statue was removed. We brought them a new image of the blessed Virgin –'

'And it was so ugly, they refused to worship it,' she reminded him. 'They in-sis-ted they have the old one back – *she* was beautiful, as old things are. And your own bishop a-greed to re-turn her to them.'

'Yes, yes, she is there too,' he admitted irritably, 'in a corner. They can have her too if they want. What is one to do, with these *paganos*?'

Doña Vera began to laugh. The pugs looked up at her, wagged the little smiling curls of their tails and settled back around her feet, happy that she was laughing. 'The Church of the Two Virgins,' she mocked him.

'Ah, I tell you,' he muttered, and lit himself a cigar, 'that is bad enough but even worse are these *aleluyas* that have arrived in our midst.'

And now the two were in complete accord. The rest of the visit was spent in the greatest cordiality in condemn-ing the Protestant missionaries who had lately begun to arrive in droves – from Kansas, from Ohio, from Iowa – with so much cash and so much in the way of food, medi-cines, clothing and tools as enticement that there was no stemming the flood of conversions.

Fray Junípero, beginning to feel the effects of the brandy and the cigar in this midday heat, sighed and comforted himself with the thought, 'What they do not know is that, in secret, these *indios* still worship the Virgin in the old way.'

Doña Vera, who was not and never had been affected by the heat, shouted out in triumph, 'The *old* way, yes! What did I tell you? Was I not right?'

He sank back in his chair, his eyelids slipping like a turtle's over his eyes, and grumbled petulantly, 'You are always right, daughter, *always*, are you not?'

Seeing she could no longer get a rise out of him, she got up briskly – what triumph did for her! – announcing, 'And now it is time for me to go riding.'

'Ah, ah,' he groaned, failing to see how anyone could choose such activity. He had no option but to get to his feet and follow her into the hall where he saw the maids setting out a blasphemous altar of paper and wire skeletons who looked to be strumming guitars and drinking tequila, on a heap of bright marigolds and other ritual objects of their pagan celebration. 'Tch, tch, tch,' he clicked his tongue thickened with brandy, and lifting up his skirts, carefully stepped around and past it. They were too occupied and excited to notice his departure.

In the library, the scholars at their tables looked up to see Doña Vera cross the courtyard, dressed now in khaki breeches, her riding boots, a hat on her head, all old, all worn, so that now they could see that legendary character in action, the European woman who had gone into the field before any other. There had been evenings at the dining table when they had dared to ask, 'What was it like then?' and 'Is it still as it was?' only to hear her snap back, 'Why not go and find out?' and then add, with a brittle laugh, 'Ah, I see. You want a van, eh, air-con-dition-ed, and plas-tic bot-tles filled with water, and med-i-cine for every mos-qui-to bite you get. No, that is *not* how I went. Now you can only see the films and read the books about it. Easy, eh? That is what mat-ters.'

The books they read in the library, however, were not written by her. She had left it to others to write them. Her legend was not reduced and restricted to print and paper.

They did not guess – glancing at them through the window as she passed, she was certain they did not guess – that she had no education beyond elementary school, that she had not been to a university or acquired a degree (other than the honorary ones that had been conferred on her later) and feared to write so much as a monograph lest it give her away. Besides, which language could she have written in? Neither English nor Spanish, both spoken languages to her, not literary ones. The only one she could write with any ease was one she would never use: she had crushed it out of herself. No tracks, no tracks.

The craftsmen on the veranda looked up from the beads they were arranging, delicately and patiently, into deer, maize and peyote symbols. They prepared to smile if she stopped to see what they were making – deer, maize, peyote . . .

She did not. Walking past, she only grimaced and waved. The craftsmen were perhaps the only people who saw that particular smile, an embarrassed, ingratiating smile no one else caused her to make.

She did turn her head and shout at the maids to bring them a carafe of *té de Jamaica*. So they smiled, bowed their heads in acknowledgement and went back to the beads in colours of sea green, quetzal blue, gold, grey and silver.

Perhaps another day they would broach the matter of a trip to the city – and escape.

She made her way down the cactus-lined path to the corral below, her boots sinking into the soft white wool of dust. She hummed to herself and switched the whip at her side to dispel the sense of guilt she felt in passing them without a word: she ought to be doing more for them, making more of an effort at marketing their wares. The truth was that few buyers ever came to the Hacienda de la Soledad. She would have to carry it all to the city to be sold, and the very thought of their wares spread out on pavements along with handbags and watches and tin toys and plastic sandals upset her, conjuring up the streets of her childhood, lined with the shops of butchers and bakers and greengrocers, with merchant fists and merchant faces inhabiting them. It was what she had struggled to escape. Roderigo was supposed to have rescued her from all that, but wasn't it what he too had been occupied in, if more grandly, as baron of silver?

She turned upon the pugs, threatening them with her whip. 'Go back, go back,' she shouted, and for a brief moment a vision from last night rose up, surrounding and nearly suffocating her again. 'You are not to fol-low, hear? Go back! Now! At once!' She slapped her whip against her thigh and when that made them cower but not turn, she kicked out her foot and caught one with the tip of her boot. It gave a squeal, the squeal of a pig facing slaughter, and that made them all turn, the curls in their tails coming undone and drooping, and flee back up the path.

Opening the gate to the corral and then shutting it carefully behind her, she saw the groom waiting with her horse, and waved, '¡Ho-la-a!' not with false joviality but with a genuine lifting and expanding of the heart and spirits at the thought of being free now and by herself again.

The groom, watching her ride out through the tall grass into the open, let out a sharp whistle. Then another, and another, just like a bird calling, at first tentatively, then confidently when it signals the passing of a storm.

Consuela came out into the courtyard above, hurriedly, and looked around to see if anyone was watching before she ran down the path to the corral.

Eric came out of his room, dragging his bag. 'I have left the key inside,' he called to Consuela, making her halt a moment. '*Adiós!*' he waved, and suddenly felt light-hearted as he let himself out of the Hacienda de la Soledad into the dirt road that would take him to the crossing with the highway where he would flag down a bus or a truck.

It was only a matter of going through the tunnel now and then he would be in the ghost town he had come to see on the other side of the mountain. He began to whistle.

Thunderheads had risen above the horizon and were mounting with swift strides through the sky, casting a shadow across the mesa and the lake as if a fisherman had flung out a net over them that softly settled. All the grasses bent, with a long, hissing breath. The *situí* birds spun out into the air, crying, '*Tuí, tuí.*' But the clouds sailed on as if they had other, larger plans and could not stop.

Eric gave up whistling as the weight of the bag and the sinking of his shoes into the dust began to tire him long before he reached the crossing. He could not help think-ing how foolish a traveller he must appear to anyone who could see him – without auto, without burro, without spouse or partner. Not that there was anyone to see. He had been told there would be many making their way to the town for *el Día de los Muertos*, but the only figure he could make out was the one on the horse down below on the mesa, slowly breasting the reeds and the rushes around the flat lake whose surface crinkled like a sheet of burnt paper.

He wondered at that figure, at the freedom it had won – of space, of movement – although from what, he had failed to discover. She had evidently sloughed off the past and emerged like some sly and secretive snake in its new skin, to continue on her way. That was what she had done, while here he was, struggling to do the reverse: retrace an old passage, and follow it to – well, what? That was yet to be discovered.

Looking down at his bag, now dragging a trail through the dust, and his reddened fingers clasping the handle, he thought there were always those who walked away, and those who did not. This had been the unsatisfactory meeting of the two, he guessed wryly.

The next time he glanced up the road the bus appeared, juddering along over the skull shapes of the cobblestones of the highway, dragging itself over them as if drawn by a pulley it was trying to resist. He began to run; he did not want to be left here for another night under her roof.

He heaved himself and his bag into the bus – it was second class and therefore stopped for whoever hailed it. He bought a ticket and found a seat on a bench at the back between a woman with a basket full of indignant chickens and a man with a bottle of beer and a beatific smile. They made room for him and he settled in.

The best way he knew to shut out the noise and the images and incidents of the journey was to think of Em. Where was she? Was she too on a journey at this moment?

Of what kind? Surely much more certain and logical than his. Em knew why she was travelling and where to, whereas he seemed to be chasing a whim, perhaps even less, merely an instinct that he must follow the tracks. Until now, he had studied history and collected data without any sense that it was essential (Em had been right to question him, repeatedly and anxiously, about his intentions). What was it for, really? Simply to add to his papers, make his contribution to what already existed? As pointless – and now he knew why he had worked without any urgency – as adding one more grain of sand to a shore where the ocean washed up more with every wave. But now that he was following the trail of his own history, tunnelling his way back into his ancestry, and the history of his ancestors, he felt for the first time the urgency – and the terror – of knowing. An urgency, and a terror, he could have shared at last with Em.

So he listened to the roar of the engine as it thundered through the tunnel in the mountain, and waited for the moment when it would emerge and he would open his eyes – to what? Would this sight, this revelation, accord him at last a certainty like a secret finally unfolded, something he could commit himself to? He remembered Em's words to him, that he would, once he was alone, discover things he could not when he was with her. He had not believed her, but they seemed now to have the ring of truth.

It was with that prospect that he emerged from the tunnel in the bus, and dismounted – an explorer on the brink of discovery. Only it was dark and a cold wind rustled through the trees in the park and he had to ask the way to an inn.

Chapter 5

We feared death, because we were men.

Bernal Díaz, *The Conquest of New Spain*, 1568

When he woke the next morning, he noticed first that the wind had stopped blowing so that, in the ringing clarity of air, whatever sound there was reverberated metallically. That was the cathedral bell, striking the hour. Befuddled with sleep, he lay listening to it, but not counting, the rings of the bell bounding out over the roofs like an iron ball. A sliver of light made its way under the curtains cunningly as a sharp knife. He was enormously grateful for both, revived by them, as if he had passed through a storm and now realised that he had survived. This is how a traveller's waking should be, he decided.

Upstairs, the tables were laid for breakfast with bright checked cloths. From the kitchen came sounds of pans being struck and stirred and fat spattering, meat briskly sizzling. The two officials from the night before were already mopping up the last of their beans and eggs with tortillas. Coffee was brought in a pot battered with much service. Eric held out his mug and let the black liquid pour in with benign normality.

Through the door that opened on to the side street, he could see a woman setting up her stall for the day's customers, unpacking her baskets and bundles, emptying them out. A hen ran by squawking, pursued by a rooster. The woman threw a corn cob at it, laughing.

A basket of rolls arrived at his table, accompanied by butter and *mermelada*.

The swing door to the kitchen banged open again and André entered. Eric caught a glimpse of the child playing in the kitchen, under the feet of the maids in their frilled aprons. André himself looked washed, fresh, energetic, perhaps a smear of grease at the corner of his mouth from his breakfast. He came to Eric's table to enquire if he had slept well, if he had plans for the day. Eric asked if he would join him for a cup of coffee and was pleased that André accepted: he had not thought that he would want to continue the conversation of last night but André seemed eager to do so, as if to correct any misapprehensions.

It was that kind of a morning, fresh, new. Water was being sluiced down the street, pans were ringing like church bells and a triumphant rooster was crowing.

Lighting cigarettes for both of them, André looped an arm over his chair and began immediately. 'Perhaps I gave you the impression that I know much about Doña Vera. It is not true. I know a little and I guess a little.'

'But she's lived here a long time?'

'Yes, but she keeps to herself. In the Hacienda de la Soledad. Well named, is it not? Her family *is* well known

– you will see its name everywhere – but she herself, not much.'

'Her family? She belongs here?'

'No, no, no, the family she married into. Her husband, a Creole, very wealthy, for many generations. They owned mines, houses, streets. When President Díaz visited, it was in their house he stayed. But they did not live here themselves. They lived in Mexico City, and Guanajuato, and Guadalajara. Doña Vera alone has chosen to live here, for many years now, you are right.'

'To start her centre for Huichol studies?'

This time André did explode into laughter. 'Who knows why? She is a person about whom many rumours go round. But yes, she did start the centre. You came to see it?'

Eric refuted any such intention. 'I had never heard of it, to tell you the truth. Nor about the Huichol. But I had learned of her connection to the mines here and my family had one as well.'

'Oh, *mein Gott.*' André slapped his forehead with mock horror and ash scattered from his cigarette. 'You did not tell her *that*? She will not have loved you if you did.'

'It's true, she did not love me at all.'

'Of course! She hated her connection to that family – to Don Roderigo – and left him many years ago.'

'But she was living on his property, and with his wealth. Weren't they divorced?'

'No, no, no. In such families that does not happen. There may be scandal about their business, their bank accounts, their dealings, but not about the family. That is not permitted. No scandal. And Doña Vera was already something of a scandal.'

Eric watched over André's shoulder as his pretty wife came out of the kitchen with a pot of coffee, and went around refilling cups, while her husband told tales to the visitor. André went on, 'No one knew anything about her, you see. And in such families it is important to know. But she was just a young woman who had fled Europe when war broke out. Who was she? Why did she flee? No one knew.'

'Many Europeans came at that time, didn't they? Refugees?'

'True.' André grew more grave, folding his hand around his coffee cup. 'Refugees from many countries and many pasts. Politics of all kinds.'

'So what were hers?'

He shrugged. 'One more mystery. Many more rumours. Some have said she was a Nazi, a collaborator who got out before it was too late. Some say the opposite – that she was in the Resistance, about to be betrayed. That is the story she herself encourages, I am told. For that reason, I think it was the opposite.'

Eric was surprised by André's shrewdness; he had not expected it. But that did not mean it was to be trusted. 'Is there proof?' he asked 'Evidence?'

'Not here. She has hidden herself very well, has she not? Who will find her here? But they say there are archives in Europe – in Austria and in Germany – where there are letters, documents that could tell us something.'

'Hasn't anyone done research into them?'

'No one over here. Perhaps in Europe – but in Europe they don't know her Mexican life. I don't think she was so important, only that she maybe knew people who were. You know? Her story has many chapters – European, Mexican, Huichol . . .'

'And what do you think of that?' Eric asked, suddenly curious about André's interest in this story.

'Of –?'

'Of walking away, leaving behind one chapter, starting another?'

André did not reply at once. He drew on his cigarette, pursing his lips and releasing spirals of smoke. Watching them uncurl and disperse in the air, Eric wondered if that was his comment. Eventually, though, he crushed his cigarette in a saucer with the name of the inn painted in curlicues on a brown glaze, and clasped his hands on the table top. Eric could see that the question had made him uncomfortable. Perhaps he was thinking of his own story, and its different chapters. He might also be thinking of his country's story. Certainly his face had taken on a melancholy look.

'I think that, on one level or another, it is what we do,' he said finally. 'People, countries. If we think about our sins, our guilt, it is a heavy baggage we carry.' He scratched his head. 'It is why, over here, people go to church so happily – every day, many times a day, whenever they pass by one. They go in, make a sign of the cross, so, pray a little, light a candle, and come out – forgiven, ready to move on.'

'And those of us who are not believers?'

André shrugged. 'Perhaps we must forgive ourselves.'

'Do you believe one can?' Eric asked in surprise.

'*No.* I think more is required, *much* more. Sacrifice, perhaps. Like in the old days – animal, material, even human.'

They thought about that: everywhere in this country one saw the stains of sacrifice; blood was inextricable from history.

'How do you know when you've sacrificed enough – goats, chickens, boys, virgins? Gold, silver, jewels? How much before you're forgiven?'

'Perhaps the priest tells you. Or you tell yourself. You forgive yourself. But that is not enough. It is others who must forgive you. You must earn it.'

'Can there be forgiveness for killing, for taking life?'

'No, I don't believe that.'

'I don't either.'

'So perhaps one must live a life of penance. Of service.'

'Do you think Doña Vera's life is that, of penance? By trying to serve the Huichol? An interesting idea. She does have them stay in her house.'

André sat back, his posture relaxing as if a certain danger had passed. He even laughed. 'A good trophy, eh? Something to show off with, no?'

Eric suddenly found that he had placed his finger on something that had troubled him. 'It is strange, but she never speaks *to* them, only *of* them – to the foreigners who are present.'

'You know why?' André's eyes were twinkling. He seemed capable of a good deal of mischief. 'I tell you why. I believe – I believe – she does not know the language! That is why. She has never learned the language! Such "experts" are to be found here, in Mexico, you know. Difficult for her to keep up the pretence. Did you not find it so?'

His laughter made his wife come over to them, with her coffee pot. 'What stories are you telling our guest?' she asked him, and stood ruffling his hair with one hand, affectionately, leaning into his shoulder. 'About the ghost who haunts our inn? Or the *bandido* who was running from the law and slept here one night, the *federales* in the next room? You see,' she told Eric, 'André is our official storyteller.'

'This is a story about a neighbour, Paola. The Queen of the Sierra down below. Eric spent a night at her place.'

'Ohh,' she said dismissively. 'I have seen that when two foreigners meet, they only want to talk about other foreigners. So much they like to hear gossip and tell gossip about themselves.'

'True,' Eric had to admit; what else had they been doing after all?

Her level, dark gaze made him feel somehow ashamed. She made him think of Em; Em would have shared her attitude. 'Actually,' he said, to change the subject, 'it isn't Doña Vera or her centre I came to see. It was really the ghost town. It doesn't look much like one,' he added, glancing out of the open door at the side street where customers were beginning to cluster around the food stall and people were going up and down with their market bags.

'Oh, today is a special day. At other times, it is empty. During the Revolution, you know, the mines collapsed and they were not revived. There is no living to be made. It is very sad.'

'But you came here to live,' Eric reminded them.

'Because there was so much space, and it was free,' Paola explained. 'My father, he came from a mining family, but he could not find work himself. He did a little on his own, like many of the people left here, but it didn't bring in enough. So when he found this house empty, its owners gone, he moved in and, with my mother's help, he started the inn.'

'Do you have enough guests to stay?' Eric could not refrain from asking.

'*Unos pocos*,' she replied. 'A few. Pilgrims come for the feast of San Francisco. Also for *el Día de los Muertos*, as you see. And now, a few artists, too – like André.'

'Is that so?'

'Oh, yes,' she said, beaming. 'He has his studio upstairs and he is painting there. You must come and see.'

André, embarrassed by her suggestion, brushed it off. 'Eric has come to see the mines, Paola. His father worked in them. Can you imagine?'

'My grandfather,' he said hastily. 'It was many years ago. Those were bad times in England. People were looking for work. I thought I would look for the graves of those who died here.'

They looked distressed now and André stood up, saying, 'You did not tell me. That is a very different reason for coming.'

'Yes, well, I'm not sure if I shall find any sign of them.'

Now both began to speak together. André wanted to draw him a map of the town on a paper napkin Paola had made available. 'Here, the plaza. Here, the *museo* –'

'Closed today because of the holiday.'

'And here the *catedral*. It is grand, built by the priest who found the first silver here. You must see it.'

'Also the grand houses around the plaza where the managers and so on lived –'

'Yes, some held banquets and balls when President Díaz visited –'

Eric assured them his grandparents could not have lived grandly at all so André drew another road on his map, the one that led up to the mines where the Cornish miners had had their cottages. 'They were called Jack, all of them – Jack. They made a football field, they played the first football in Mexico –'

But, they admitted together, there was little left to see. The *palenque*, the *plaza de toros*, abandoned. 'You see, it *is* a ghost town. In ruins.'

That, Eric said, was what he had come to see.

'Only today is a festival so it comes to life. You have never seen this festival of the dead?'

'We do have one kind of like it at home,' Eric reluctantly divulged. 'Hallowe'en, the night before All Saints' Day.'

'You do? Ohh?'

He tried to describe it to them, the pumpkins carved into lanterns, the children going up and down the street at night, dressed in costumes and masks to beg for candy – but gave up in the face of their incomprehension. 'I was always frightened of it myself,' he confessed. 'I used to hide, not go out.'

'Oh, but here it is not like that. We scatter the petals of the *zempasuchíl*, on our doorsteps, to help the dead find their way home, and put their photographs out so they can see they have come to the right house, and candles to see the way because if they do not, they will have to light their fingers and burn,' Paola explained. 'Also copal, incense and flowers with a strong scent.'

'And food with a strong aroma,' André prompted her.

'Oh yes, and after the dead have eaten, that aroma will be gone because the dead will have taken away its spirit.'

'To last them a whole year.'

'And for the *angelitos*, the little children who died, we put out little things – little pieces of chocolate, chiclets, peanuts, and of course *azúcar* – sugar birds and lambs. If we make *sopa*, or stew, it is mild for the children, not spicy.'

'Families say they can hear the dishes clinking when the children are there,' André broke in.

'And among the *campesinos*, the peasants, people put out brooms and tortilla presses for their daughters and spades and hoes for their sons so in the world they have gone to, they can continue the lives they had here.'

That sounded so terribly sad to Eric that he wondered now if, as a child, he had not sensed the shadow behind the Hallowe'en masquerade, a shadow others chose to ignore, cast by the gnomon between night and day, life and death. It wavered before him once again, and he was unsettled and had to make an effort to listen to what the young pair so animatedly told him.

'On this day you visit homes where you knew the ones who died, and you bring offerings, and stay to eat with the family.'

'You must do that. There are stories told about what happens to people who don't. Tell him.'

'Yes, one man who did not believe all this, he went out drinking, all night long. When he walked home, in the morning, he saw a crowd of dead people returning to their world, and his parents were there too. They were empty-handed. Others were taking back armfuls of offerings and his parents had only clay in their hands and it was burning. When he returned home, he fell ill and died.'

'But the dead do not always like to go back. The *angelitos*, who come at midday on the thirty-first of October, have to leave on the first of November, at noon. Then the elders arrive and must return on the second. At three o'clock fireworks will be lit as a signal for them to leave.

Also, a priest will walk through our town, ringing a bell and chanting. When the dead hear that, they leave for the *panteón*, and we go too, to wash and clean and decorate the tombs, make them ready to receive them.'

'You should go to the *panteón* to see this. It is at the top of the road – in the cemetery on the mountain. It is a good day you have chosen to visit your countrymen who lived here once.'

Yes, Eric assured them, shaking off the shadow of that old fear, that was what he would do and now he would set off before it grew hotter.

Suddenly the dining room with its bright checked cloths, the kitchen with its clinking sounds, the chatter and laughter of the maids, passed into another mood. Everyone, everything seemed to gather around as if they shared what he was surely thinking, and feeling, on this day. '*Adiós*,' they called, and watched him go.

Eric came out of the inn by the front door so that he could cross again the square where he had arrived in the dark and see by daylight the casuarina trees that had made the sound of a stormy sea outside his window all night.

A man in a straw hat was sweeping the paths clean with a long twig broom. The dust swirled around in the beams that slanted through the trees and made the sunlight seem hazy and soft like very fine, silken fur.

The store where he had stopped last night to ask for directions was now doing brisk business in breakfast rolls; people were coming by to help themselves from the trays with tongs and filling their baskets. The air smelt of biscuits.

Eric had the map drawn for him by André on a paper

napkin and his backpack was still light on his shoulders. The Cathedral appeared to be on another, higher level: he could see its dome from here, above the flat-topped roofs that rose in tiers. He made his way towards it up a steep lane where booths were being set up to offer the holidaymakers what they might need for the celebration: tallow candles and buckets filled with amaranth, marigolds and gladioli, trays full of sugar skulls and freshly baked rolls, sprinkled with coloured sugar, the *pan de muertos*. Since visitors had come into town, even the shops behind the booths were taking advantage of the extra custom, and putting out displays of ladies' underwear, leather belts and sandals, plastic and aluminium kitchenware. Women had set up their stalls and were flipping tortillas, stirring gravies in earthenware pots, serving the men who sat waiting on benches. A dog ran past, followed by a whole tribe of them, their tails aloft like flags. Donkeys laboured uphill with loads of firewood, edging Eric into the drain alongside.

Then there was the flight of stairs to climb, even steeper and stonier than the lane, and beggars had posted themselves along it as in some medieval painting – the old women with their heads wrapped up in black shawls, younger ones with sleeping babies tied up in *rebozos* strapped to them, sightless beggars playing reedy mouth organs, lame ones, ancient ones and infants, chanting, caps and palms of hands held out. One had to make one's way past them as though this were Calvary itself before one could reach the sudden open space of the plaza and, soaring from there into a sky that shouted out light, the great rose-pink Cathedral of carved *cantera* stone. It must have been visible for miles to anyone who approached over the baked, brown hills that lay all around. Built to the glory of God – or to the mines and the silver that had once been hidden in them? It was for the latter his grandfather had come certainly, yet he would never have set foot in the Cathedral; to a Cornishman it would have represented medieval ignorance and superstition, backward, frightening – Eric felt sure of that.

This was clearly not what it meant to the people who were streaming into the building, and Eric, shading his eyes from the glare and wishing he had a straw hat to wear, lowered himself on to a bench to watch them from the shade of an *allée* of laurel trees: an old woman in black carrying an armful of calla lilies like a bridal bouquet, a boy and a girl holding hands and smiling smiles of hopeful, timid love, an old man in cotton trousers held up by string and the rope sandals of a peasant, inching his way on his knees across the cobbles to the flight of rose-pink stairs, then crawling up them while a young woman with an expression carved as if in stone, like a saint's, followed him with his hat in her hands.

A barefoot bootblack with a toolbox strung over his shoulders circled Eric imploringly, throwing covetous looks at his dust-caked boots, making Eric rise uneasily to his feet and decide there was no reason why he should not go into the Cathedral. A thin dog that had been sleeping under the bench was disturbed, began to scratch itself furiously, then came limping along behind him. Together they made their way up the stairs that were long, curved and soft under their feet, and Eric went through the carved oak doors into the echoing, coffin-dark interior, leaving the dog behind.

The darkness had a kind of gelid solidity to it, a thickness as of blood, or drugged sleep. Here and there a flake of gold or silver glinted when someone struck a match and lit a candle, giving Eric a faint glimmering of the proportions of the place. He made his way carefully up an aisle to the side, taking in the sight of the saints in their glass cases, pierced with arrows or with swords, bleeding into satin skirts with tinsel fringes or garlands of paper roses. Finally he arrived where Saint Francis was seated upon a golden throne, his roughly woven, dark garment stitched with myriads of silver tokens as tiny as minnows – legs, arms, hands and eyes – attached with safety pins by the devout and the desperate. Out of the muddy colouring of the walls, gleams of pink and gold murals revealed themselves like tantalising glimpses of an improbable paradise.

The stone tiles under his feet had been rubbed soft and uneven by centuries of shuffling footsteps, and when Eric paused, he saw the old man had finally arrived on his knees and was making genuflections in all four directions, one after the other, meticulously, while his daughter, if that was who she was, went up to the altar to light a candle.

A kind of indistinct murmur congealed into a single, massed hum and Eric guessed it was the prayers and confessions being mumbled by all assembled in the comfortingly dark shadows. Remembering the morning's conversation, he wondered if all the confessions and all the penance for the world's sins were not being released here, in the murky darkness, and humming around him in an endless spiral. In the bright, bleak chapels of the north, guilt and sin were not permitted, but they seemed to have gathered here for refuge and to live on, an unquiet, numinous and murmurous life in the forgiving dark. The past was alive here – crepuscular and underground, but also palpable.

Without meaning to make any gesture of the sort, he found himself following the woman to the tray from which she had picked a candle to light, and selecting two himself. Taking his cue from her, he went up to the altar and lit them from the candles already lit and flaming there, then stuck the first, and after that the second, into a bed of warm, melting wax, saying aloud as he did so, his grandparents' names: 'David Rowse.' 'Betty Jennings.'

After wavering a bit, the flames sprang up, brightly and playfully, each a wheel of bright spokes, blinding him. He stepped backwards, and as he did so, he heard laughter, the laughter of a young girl, ringing out clear and light-hearted in the dark.

He twisted around to see who it could be.

PART III

Betty Departs

And next morning we came to a broad causeway and continued our march . . . And we saw all those cities and villages built in the water . . . and we were astounded . . . (These) seemed like an enchanted vision . . . Some of our soldiers asked if it were not all a dream . . . I say again that I stood looking at it, and thought no land like it would ever be discovered in the whole world . . .

Bernal Díaz, *The Conquest of New Spain,* 1568

Chapter 6

It was Betty who was laughing, running up the wet
garden path between the dripping fuchsias and bursting
into the house to tell her sisters of the letter she had
had from Davey Rowse asking her to marry him – go
to Mexico and marry him! Gertie and Sarah stopped
their washing and ironing, their sweeping and cleaning,
wrapped their hands up in their aprons, and laughed too,
thinking she had gone mad and, laughing, she declared
that was how she also felt and it was a grand feeling.

In 1910, on a day of high wind and leaping waves and
the stink of fish rotting in the sun and on the sand, Betty
Jennings of Delabole, Cornwall, came off the boat *Mary*

Ward with the Hammer family that had engaged her to be a maid for their children during the voyage from Liverpool to Veracruz. The sea was so rough at high tide on that glittering morning, she had to be carried to shore on the shoulders of a Mexican who waded through the waves as through silver fish-scales. She shaded her eyes and saw palm trees along the beach and women in long skirts and white blouses with baskets of fish and fruit on their heads.

'It's just like in a painting,' she wrote to her sisters and her father who sat nursing his arthritic wrists and knees by a fire in the cottage at the edge of the quarries. It was the house where Betty was born and had lived till she promised her hand to Davey Rowse. They had met at a service in a Methodist chapel he had come to one Sunday before he set off to work in the silver mines of Mexico like so many others who had lost their jobs when the tin mines went out of business. Then he heard that the Hammer family who lived in a grand house up the hill from Padstow was returning to Mexico after the birth of another child and needed a girl to help on the voyage. They would pay good money for 'a willing girl, healthy and clean'. Betty was that and more as she presented herself on their doorstep in her Sunday dress, for she brought with her a letter from the chapel school in Delabole praising her diligence in studies, the neatness of her penmanship and her satisfactory grasp of arithmetic. When she came out to her father who waited in the cart by the gate, she could tell him she had been engaged.

She had young Tobias and Ned to teach their letters and numbers, and baby May to take care of while Mrs Hammer promenaded on the deck in fine weather and wilted on her bunk in the cabin when it was rough. Betty proved to have good sea legs and was not sick once even if sometimes a little pale. Still, she was extremely happy to step on to sand, frothing with foam and brittle with crushed shells and, she later told Davey, had never before known that the world was so wonderful a place.

They did not stay long in Veracruz. Mrs Hammer could never remove her linen handkerchief from her nose for the smells from the open drains that ran through the city, keeping her in mind of the dread '*vómito*' that had claimed so many lives, and she feared for her children's health. She would not let Betty take them out of the enclosed courtyard of the hotel where the mass of flowers in full bloom and the lemons and oranges on the trees provided some cover for the smells, so that all Betty saw of the city was on the carriage ride to the railway station where they embarked for Mexico City.

Travelling through the great basin of arid land beyond which hills of mauve and ochre rose and fell into fissures of violet and indigo as endlessly as the waves of the ocean, Betty was made breathless by the vast space and by the snow-topped volcanoes that appeared and disappeared like fickle moons in the sky. 'A volcano covered in snow –' she never ceased to marvel at that. She held the baby May wrapped in a shawl and looked out and imagined she could see Davey Rowse come riding on a steed to meet her. She lifted the corner of the baby's shawl to conceal the flush in her cheek.

From Mexico City, Betty wrote to her father and sisters on the fine white letter paper given her by the school-mistress at the chapel school as a parting present:

'The Hammers have a house here that is even grander than the one they have at home in Padstow. It is on two floors around a big open court with a fountain. The rooms all have a porch running outside them and there are flowers growing everywhere and cages full of song-birds. They have a carriage of their own and in the evenings we go for rides in Chapultepec Park and along the broad road they say is just like a street in Paris, with marble statues and fountains and rows of trees, but I'm certain Paris never saw such sunshine as we have here every day.'

Another time she wrote of a party the Hammers gave:

'Mrs Hammer let me have a gown of her own to wear, light blue with roses round the hem, she said after three babies she could not wear that any more,' and music was played and old English songs sung by the guests around a piano in the big salon. Then they began to dance and she went up to watch them from a gallery above till she fell asleep.

She described the hot chocolate brought to her room in the morning by a maid and the basket of fruit placed on the dresser for her to pick grapes and bananas from whenever she chose.

Then she wrote:

'Now Davey has come to fetch me and my bag is all packed again and we are to take the train north. We will go straight to the chapel from the boarding house and be married there. Davey says the chapel is just like the one at home and we will have his Cornish friends as witnesses. Mrs Moran who runs the boarding house will give me away, Father, and she is like a mother to Davey so you need have no fears. I will think of all of you at home in

Cornwall and in my heart I will be with you even if I am here in Mexico. Mrs Hammer gave me the blue gown with the pink roses as a wedding dress and also a pretty workbox of inlaid wood in which to keep pins and buttons and needles and threads to keep Davey and me neat and tidy, she said.'

They travelled northwards through the Sierra Madre where even the valleys were higher than any mountains Betty had ever known, and the air was as sharp as glass cut into splinters, flashing. The earth stretched out pale and dun except where the maguey grew here and there between red, raw rocks, spear-tipped around the shooting central stalk. In the evening, darkness spread in pools at the bottom of the valleys, then rose up over the hills so that what had been pastel earlier became gradually sombre as night.

Occasionally they saw in the distance the white bell tower and dome of a church in the shadow of a mountain, or a man riding a burro bareback across the valley, or a pair of wild horses grazing where a hidden *barranco* was marked by a sheath of green.

Betty did not say if what she saw awed or frightened or enchanted her but she did, in every line, express her trust in Davey and her joy in being with him.

He had no close family to whom he wrote of his feelings.

'We travelled three days and nights and when we arrived we were little better than dust mops and badly in need of hot water and soap. This we did get at Mrs Moran's boarding house and ate a good Cornish tea with saffron cake she had herself baked. I wished I had been able to stay up and ask her the many questions I have but I was so tired that I went up to bed and slept a longer, deeper sleep than any I have ever had.

'Mrs Moran, on taking me into the village to buy provisions, told me that when the first "Cornish Jacks" came to work in the mines, the villagers had received them with the ringing of bells and thronged the church to offer prayers for their success, but that many proved a disgrace with their drinking and fighting, and some had to be sent back! Of course if anyone in her house is found drinking, she has them leave. Then she showed me the store that is run by the Company where I might buy whatever I need for my house. The prices seemed to me high but she explained that was because all the goods come a long way from elsewhere. Nor is there much stock but it will do, I'm sure.'

A few days later Betty Jennings and Davey Rowse were married by Edgar Butler, a lay preacher, before a small Methodist congregation gathered to witness the ceremony. Mrs Moran of the boarding house provided the wedding breakfast, Davey having been a lodger of long standing and always an abstemious, quiet and well-behaved young man, unlike many others in the town. She gave Betty a china butter dish from her collection, scarcely used, and a set of baskets, quite new, that she would find useful.

In a letter to Miss Frances at the chapel school, Betty described her new home in detail:

'We have moved into our own home in a row on the hillside amongst the other miners' cottages. They are not so unlike the ones at home in Cornwall, except they have red tiled roofs and the walls are as coloured as a rainbow – bright blue next to yellow, and pink or orange next to green. The windows that open on to the street have wooden shutters and iron grilles too. At the back there are no windows but only doors that open on to a courtyard. It is not so grand as the Hammers' house in Mexico City and there is no fountain but there is a stone trough for washing in, and along the wall are trees with lemons and oranges and a dark fruit like a pear that they call the avvycado. The kitchen is quite small and a bit dark, not like the bright sunny one at home, but Davey has put in all the shelves I need and pretty painted tiles around the sink so it is a treat to do the dishes here.'

She wrote too, of 'the boy who fetches water on the back of a little donkey and pours it into a big stone filter by the door where Davey has set up a wooden frame to hold it', and of the Mexican women who 'carry baskets of laundry down the street to the foot of the hill where they scrub their clothes together in stone troughs which must be a lot nicer than doing it alone at home. Then they spread them out on the rocks by a little stream and while they wait for them to dry, they sit talking and combing out each other's long black hair and plaiting it with bright ribbons. I wish I could paint it all for you, it would make a pretty picture.'

To her sisters she proudly reported:

'I baked my first batch of pasties today in a little clay oven and Davey said the men at the mine would envy him. Now he wants me to bake him a saffron cake but there is no yeast to be had. Mrs Moran told me the women use "*pulque*" instead. That is a kind of spirits they make out of the juice of the cactus. I don't like to touch it but better to eat it in bread than drink it in the tavern, for sure.'

Those who read her letters might have thought her a child playing at keeping house but that was because there were aspects of her life she omitted to mention. She did not write of watching the Cornish children go up the hill to the little school run by the sisters Lily and Minnie Bennett of Helston who had come out to keep house for their brother only to find, on their arrival, that he had died in a mining accident and, lacking the money for a return passage, stayed to make a living for themselves, with the help of the community. Nor did she write of the drunken brawls in town or the sights to be seen outside the tavern on a Saturday night. Sundays were not a day on which it was wise to step out of the house either. The miners, released from work on that one day of the week, revelled with the money they had made, spending it at cock fights where fortunes were gambled away, and in the taverns. By nightfall the streets were littered with the drunk and on Monday morning there was a surly, taciturn return to work. Once again the whistle blew to mark the shifts at the mine and the miners' boots tramped up the cobblestoned way to work, to Betty's relief. She missed prayer meetings at the Methodist chapel, for such gatherings could only be held on those Sundays that Edgar Butler was visiting their village. Instead, she sang hymns to herself while washing up or baking pasties for Davey to take in his lunch box to the mine.

There was her first scorpion, an occasion that made her scream. Davey was at work, and the little maid, Lupe, swept it out with a broom, laughing. But then there was a second, a third and a fourth, making her fearful, wondering where the next one would drop from or crawl out from, and once there was a whole nest of infant scorpions, so tiny that they seemed like little red ants clinging to their mother's back, falling off, scattering in all directions because of Betty's frenzy.

Davey, tired, his hands raw, his hair dusty, sat at the table, watching her, and after a bit said flatly, 'We all live here together, Betty – the scorpions, and us. It's home to them, home to us.'

His words silenced her screaming and made her stare at him in bewilderment.

All around there were sights and sounds that nothing had prepared her for – the rough wooden crosses erected on hilltops, to her mind like gallows, and sinister. Who had climbed up there to do that, and why? A donkey braying on the hillside, sounding like a rusty pump being worked up and down, up and down, with a vengeance. Not a sound that could be ignored or shut out, any more than the crowing of roosters in the dark, long before daylight, one crow leading to the next, from hill to hill and village to village around the valley till sunrise when sound merged with light, ringing and blazing together.

The turkey buzzards hovering in the sky, their wingtips like fingertips tilted against the currents as they circled, languidly, watching out for a lamb that had fallen down a *barranco* or a mule that had drawn its last load and spilt its guts on the stony paths, too weak to resist their beaks or talons.

Betty would climb the slope of the hill behind the cottage and sit there on a rock, clasping her knees and watching for signs of life in the flat plain below and find herself waiting for the sight of the train that made its way slowly to the foot of the hill to unload machinery or timber to be taken by carts up to the mines or to be loaded with ore for the smelters. As it crawled around the boulders and hillocks of the plain, now appearing and now disappearing from sight, Betty played with the gravel at her fingers and found herself chanting the rhyme she had heard the village children sing, '*Tucu-tucu, tiqui-taca*,' and no one could have said if she was so pensive because she was thinking of her arrival, or her departure.

There were aspects of their world that were too strange to be conveyed to those at home – the way the day started at the mine, for instance: how the men lined up in pairs, had their names entered in a big ledger and took the tools and powder handed them, then followed the overseer to the entrance where they stopped in front of a crucifix that hung there to make a sign of the cross. Singing the Ave Maria, they entered the mine, the voices of those who went in first growing fainter as the ones who followed sounded louder, then fainter too, as if they were descending a well. On a landing below they had erected an image of the saint they worshipped, the saint of *trabajadors*, workmen, decorated with fresh flowers or branches, and they would light candles to him before going in different directions to start work. When Davey first described the scene to Betty, she was shocked by such popish rites but he assured her that the Cornishmen took no part in them and that, on emerging from the mine at the end of the day, it was their own good Methodist hymns they sang on the way home.

She did write of the market that was held in the open on Saturdays and to which she liked to go. She could have obtained the goods she needed at the Company store as the other miners' wives did and was in fact taken along to it sometimes by Mrs Moran and sometimes by their neighbour's wife, Ida Hoskin, a pale sad woman whose husband was a heavy drinker, a champion wrestler and a brute. But Betty drooped in their company, finding Ida Hoskin 'boring' and Mrs Moran 'a bit too fussy and old-fashioned', enquiring into her household and housekeeping habits as if to make sure Betty was taking good care of Davey, her favourite. She much preferred her visits to the Saturday market with Lupe although she had twinges of guilt when she thought that Lupe ought to be in school instead. She fantasised about giving her lessons – but in what, English? To what end? Have her memorise the Lord's Prayer when she could tell her rosary as well? Besides, she appeared to know all she needed to know as she bargained over the price of eggs or picked the plumpest chicken out of a basket of indignant brown feathers and sadly limp necks and beaks. So Betty assuaged her guilt by buying ribbons for her plaits or a sack of oranges for her to take home to her family.

Loaded with their market baskets, they found the way back up the hill much slower. Betty preferred not to walk along the dirt road where mules and carts churned up the dust. She let Lupe take her along a path over the stony hillside that led past the potter's hut, a poor thing of adobe with a sheet of tin for a roof, and outside, in a corral fenced with thorns, his herd of three goats and a cow, and a brick kiln. If he was firing his pots, a thread of smoke unspooled from it, but he did not do this often and on most days he was to be seen wandering in the gullies below with his cattle, searching for something to graze them on. There was not much, the vegetation had long ago been destroyed by the mines and their effluents. Sometimes he could be seen all the way down where the stream ended in a shallow, stagnant pool with mesquite trees standing in it, grey-legged and ghostly. While his beasts waded into the water and seemed to be imbibing moisture through their hides and hooves, he collected clay in a pail and dragged it uphill after them. Then he would disappear into his hut and it would be his wife who would go out with the cattle and return with branches of mesquite or cacti that had died and turned to skeletons that she would feed into the fire in the kiln. That was when the smoke emerged and announced that pots were being fired for the Saturday market.

Sometimes he even glazed them so that they looked like the burnished chestnuts Betty had collected at home with her sisters in the autumn. He would draw patterns on them, swirling free shapes, all in a kind of dark dye. Betty wondered where the paint came from, she had seen none in the market. One day she saw him up at the mine, his ragged trousers held up by string and his bare feet so calloused that they looked like shoe soles, picking his way along the tracks where wagons travelled with loads of ore. He had a rusty can in his hand in which he was collecting cinders that he bent down to pick. Perhaps that was what he ground on those flat stones outside his hut, mixed in a pot and used for paint. A twig of mesquite would have done for a paintbrush, she thought. That must be how he drew the patterns along the rims of his bowls and, occasionally, if the spirit moved him or he had enough paint, he might even do a funny sketch of a woman taking a pig to market or a fish with a mermaid at the end of its fishing line.

Those were the ones that Betty looked out for if she found he had brought in a consignment to spread out on a rush mat at the market. She greeted him, eager to know him, but his face remained in the shadow of his sombrero and he said nothing as she picked out a soup bowl or a mug for coffee and paid him. Lupe stood with her hands twisted in her apron, embarrassed. She tried to direct her mistress's attention to the store where china cups could be had, with flowers painted on them, the kind she had seen in other English homes. And here was her mistress buying cheap earthenware from the village potter, losing face thoughtlessly.

Curiously, it was the same expression Betty caught on Davey's face when she gave him his tea in such a mug. Clearly he did not think it fit for a miner.

Chapter 7

Labouring constantly in dark passages, secluded from
the world, hardens their characters . . . and they are
inclined to superstition and fanaticism. They believe
in mountain-spirits and hear them hammering far
down in the bowels of the earth. They also have presen-
timents, and refuse to admit women in the mine, as
the ore would then disappear.

Carl Sartorius, *Mexico and the Mexicans*, 1859

The Cornish miner had his own version of sprite, the
tommy knocker which gave him a warning of a cave-in.

A. C. Todd, *The Search for Silver*, 1977

There were times when Davey did make clear to Betty
what he thought of her free ways. There was the occasion when the circus came to town, one of the many small,
mangy circuses that travelled from village to village with
its creaking wagons and brass band. The striped tent went
up in a dusty field, the cages with their shabby lions and
bears drawn into a circle. The hurdy-gurdy played its
tunes excruciatingly, and spun sugar billowed out of a
booth in a sweet cumulus cloud of livid pink. A man in
a clown's costume rode a donkey through the town, shouting, 'See el Gran Hernandez pull a loaded wagon with
his teeth! See la Bella Isadora ride a mighty elephant!'
and Betty grew as excited as a child, as Lupe. 'Oh, let's

go,' she cried because, at home, wouldn't she have caught her friends Agnes's and Sally's hands and gone running? But it appeared that in Mexico a Cornish woman could not do that, go down to the Indian village and sit there with brown Mexican crowds. Davey's appalled look made that clear.

It was only the woman known to them as Tough Tansy, wife to the carpenter at the works and mother of five, who dressed her children up in their best and took them down as bold as could be, asking no one for permission. She kept her chin up and marched down the lane, herding her brood before her like a flock of goslings, and calling out to the women who watched from their doorways, 'We're going to the circus – to see the Gran Hernandez eat fire and Issydora ride the ellyphant, aren't we, chicks? Come along!'

Davey said that it served Fred Barnstaple right for picking up a woman here in Mexico for a wife instead of fetching a proper one from Cornwall, and when Betty sulked over the sink and the dishes, he pointed out to her all the social activities provided for the miners' families by the Company, 'like the picnic on the Duke of Cornwall's birthday'. He was taken aback by Betty's fiery outburst at that.

'Oh yes,' she said, hands on her hips, 'that's the one day your fine manager and his wife think of the miners up on the hill. Give us a tea treat with bacon sandwiches and feel proud when they see us fall on them like beggars. Then they can go back to their Casa Grande where none of us has ever so much as set foot.'

'Now, Betty, I didn't think you'd care to visit them.'

'I don't,' she said, stamping her foot, 'I don't. That

is not what I meant and you know it, Davey Rowse.'

But she gave her family an account of the occasion that sounded happy enough. 'Did you ever think,' she wrote, 'that here on a mountain in Mexico we would be celebrating the Duke of Cornwall's birthday?' They had been taken in wagons decorated with streamers down the steep hillside to a ledge where the picnic had been spread out under a great mesquite tree and games arranged for the children, races for the adults. When the sun began to sink, Davey came and pulled Betty to her feet, asking her to come and look at the view with him. It was one of those rare days when work and responsibility did not seem to weigh on him and make him dour, and Betty, delighted to see it, agreed.

They walked down to the edge where the land fell away in a sudden precipice to the valley and a lake where egrets stepped among the reeds, herons spread their wings to dry and pelicans sailed along as if sliding across glass. He was pointing out the different birds to her when she noticed a large solitary hacienda built against the flank of the mountain already in shadow and so dark as to be barely discernible.

'And that?' she asked.

'Oh, that was a convent built by the Spanish priests who came to convert the Indians. The Mexicans threw them out after the the War of Independence.'

'So, is it empty? Did no one move in?'

'Actually, the Company did. They bought it and turned it into a kind of guest house for people on the board when they come to see the mines. 'Course, no one does. Come out here to the back of beyond to see the muck their fortunes come from? Not them,' Davey said, looking at her because he knew she would approve of his tone. 'It just lies empty. But when the President of Mexico came to open our electrical installation, he stayed there and the owners threw a banquet for him. They had chefs come from Mexico City to prepare his meals,' Davey went on, providing the details he knew Betty enjoyed so much, 'and an orchestra to play for him so he could dance with the ladies. Then he came up here to the mines and they lined the road with lanterns and trees hung with paper flowers. They lit bonfires on every hilltop and had a fireworks display to beat all fireworks. Just as if he was a king.'

'A king in a fairy story,' Betty said wonderingly. 'We should go there one day.' Glancing over her shoulder at the gathering under the tree, she added, 'Just us, you and me.'

He smiled and plucked a grass stalk to chew on. 'How? We'd have to get a horse to take us. Shall we ride a horse together, Mrs Rowse?'

The picture amused her. 'Let's.'

Holding hands, they strolled back to where the gathering had begun to sing Cornish songs and when they got back and rejoined them, a toast was drunk to the Duke – beer for the men, lemonade for the women and children. Then Betty helped the women pick up and fold and tidy away and the men got the wagons ready to take them back.

The occasion for that excursion never did arise, and shortly afterwards Davey forbade Betty to go for walks alone on evenings when he was kept late at the mine, and he actually laid down the limits beyond which she must not go, even with Lupe.

Betty was puzzled. 'What do you think might happen if I did?'

'I cannot tell and that is what I don't care for, not to know what might happen. All I know is it's not safe.'

'And who told you that?'

'There's talk,' he said. 'Don't think everyone is so friendly as you think.'

It displeased her that he should be suspicious of the people they lived among and whom she knew to be friendly and kind for they unfailingly wished her a '*Buenos días*' and a '*Buenas tardes*' when they passed her and never pulled a face or made a gesture that could be thought hostile. It made her wonder at Davey's new attitude – he was often dour but never unfair – and she demanded a reason for it.

He explained that there had been trouble at the mine: one of the *mineros*, Julio, was found to have gone down the hill into town to buy kerosene for his lantern and corn for his family at the general store, not at the Tienda de Reya run by the Company. The manager, a Scotsman named MacDuff, had him hauled up and warned. When he defied the manager and did it again, saying he would go wherever the prices were fair, he was discharged and a wave of anger and resentment went through the community that Betty imagined was so harmonious. Did not all the men play football together, Scots and Cornish and Mexican? Were they not equally excited about the Centennial celebrations to come? Now this was shown to be a sham, nothing but a front for what was unacceptable.

Putting down her knife and fork, she exploded, 'And isn't any of you standing up for him? For shame!'

When Davey kept silent and did not openly agree with her, she went on, 'Don't you think it's wrong? These poor people being made to make over what they earn back to the Company? By *order*?'

'It's not as simple as that, Betty.'

'Oh, but it is,' she insisted, 'it is.'

In Mexico City the Centennial of the Revolution was inaugurated by President Díaz. In their town they heard of banquets at the Palacio Nacional where French cuisine was prepared for the guests and an orchestra of more than a hundred musicians played the President's favourite waltz, '*El Abandonado*', under thousands of electric lights. At one such ball, he announced his intention to stand for a ninth term as President. At the same occasion he handed out ninety-nine-year concessions of copper, oil and land to the Americans, Morgan, Guggenheim, Rockefeller and Hearst.

Such news reassured all the foreigners who had begun to grow worried and so celebrations came even to their dusty scrapheap of a town. The miners and their families were taken down to hear the *grito*, the stirring call to independence that had been made by the priest Miguel Hidalgo way back in 1810. It was read out now on the balcony of the town hall by the mayor in his polished and buttoned and gleaming best. A band played, there was a parade of floats from which beauties in Spanish dress tossed roses to the crowds, buntings and streamers blew from every lamp-post and, in the evening, there were fireworks in the plaza for which the entire town turned out, Mexican and Cornish alike. When they came to an end, in drifting parasols of smoke, the night sky, clearing, revealed a pale band that seemed to be the ghost of a streaking rocket. Only it did not speed away and die. It remained because it was Halley's Comet. Everyone had heard what it portended but no one wished to say on that night. Even the mines were shut and silent, no whistle blew to remind them they were there. Instead, all turned to tables loaded with great earthenware bowls filled with food simmering in sauces and gravies.

Betty turned away and asked to be taken home. Davey was concerned because it was not like her to refuse anything unusual or pleasurable. He suggested, at home, that she have a glass of milk or a slice of fruit. Pulling a face at the pineapple in the bowl on the table, she said, 'I'd give a lot for a fresh juicy apple off a tree.'

'Why, what's wrong?' Davey asked in surprise. 'I never heard you say no to a pineapple before.'

She merely shook her head. The truth was that she had even stopped going to the market – its sights and aromas now made her feel quite ill. There had been the time she had wandered by mistake into a lane lined with booths where herbal remedies were sold. The bunches of dried herbs and roots had not been so bad but there were objects that mystified her – racoon tails, squirrel pelts, dried puffer and devil fish, even a stuffed alligator and a string of emerald hummingbirds. These were all very dead and harmless but under the tables some sacks moved with mysterious life and the tail of an iguana protruded from one, the snout of an armadillo from another, making her rush away, with Lupe laughing at her squeamishness.

Davey reacted with his usual equanimity, explaining these were the ingredients used by the witch doctors to

134

cure various sicknesses and ailments. 'There's no hospital around here, you know.'

'I hope I'm not ever ill here, Davey,' she said, shuddering.

'Just don't go there again,' he advised reasonably.

'I won't,' she said, but there had been the boy who had followed her, holding in one hand a lit candle, in the other a bottle. When he saw her looking at them, he held the lit candle under the bottle and that was when she saw it contained a live scorpion. Shocked as she was, she could not tear herself away and watched, in horror, the scorpion raise its tail over its head and sting itself to death. Laughing into her face, the boy held out his hand and demanded a peso before Lupe could push him away.

She neither told Davey nor wrote home of it.

The tempo, the tenor of life on the mountain and around the mine began to change as news filtered in – that a General Madero had declared an end to thirty years of Porfirio Díaz's rule, that the President had fled to the United States. All of this was incredible to those who had not known anything or anyone else in power for all or most of their lives. Then stories began to buzz like swarming bees, of Emiliano Zapata in the south, and Pancho Villa in the north. Zapata had once cleaned horse dung from floors of Carrara marble in President Díaz's stables, it was said, and now led a troop of mounted Indians against the president's troops. As for Pancho Villa, he was never without a gun at all, saying, 'For me the war began when I was born.' New heroes for new times: their stories began to acquire a reality, and immediacy.

Then the *mineros* began to disappear from their own mine, without a word. When the manager sent for them, it was to find their huts abandoned, thorn bushes stacked in the open doorways. They had been recruited – some by the rebels, others by the federals – and gone to fight for their country. Their women had gone with them, *soldaderas* of the Revolution. The village on the hill below the Cornishmen's cottages had only a few old people left in it, to mind the children, and some whining, hungry dogs.

The railway trains that President Díaz had only lately inaugurated still creaked and rattled over the vast plains of Mexico. They had escorts of armed guards, but were watched by men in sombreros from behind the red and purple rocks of the Sierra. Whistles sounded in the stillness, accentuating the silence.

Tiqui-taca, rucu-raca . . .

Then there was a night when the hills, usually silent mounds of darkness, echoed with a sudden volley of shots, shocking and splintering. When the men went out to see what was happening, they saw flames leaping up over a neighbouring mine on a distant hilltop – it might have been a celebratory bonfire. At dawn the news came that the rebels, the *insurgentes*, had looted the warehouse, emptied the vaults and, after tying up whoever they found on the premises, vanished along with the Company's mules. There was panic at the news. '*Insurgentes*?' people asked. 'From where?' and some went over to release the trussed manager and supervisor and assess the damage. A party of federals rode into the town soon after – grim, dusty, saddled officers of the government – asking for leads. Had anyone seen the rebels? No? They were warned to be on guard and report.

Everyone watched constantly. By daylight, a cloud of dust raised along a path could give away the approach of troops – rebels or federals – but by night there was no such sign; they could only strain their ears for the telltale clatter of hooves or a shot and the hiss that followed a bullet. Men stayed up at night, smoking, drinking, playing cards, waiting.

They were to wait for the hoot of an owl. 'An *owl*?' Betty asked when told. It would be a man, Davey informed her, with the message: '*La muerte viene con el tecolate.*' Betty thought this the foolishness of grown men playing boys' games. 'Death comes with an owl!' she sniffed.

Older men who had been in the mining towns in the desert and the Sierra for decades already recalled the raids of the Comanches and the Apaches. This, too, made Betty sniff. 'Comanches! Scalp-hunters! They've been hearing too many of those Wild West stories, I think.'

Ignoring her scorn, when he was put on a night shift, Davey engaged a boy, Lupe's brother, to keep guard over the house. Betty could not sleep for the awareness of his presence on their doorstep.

She begged Davey to send him away. 'Then I'll have to send you to San Luis Potosí for safety. Some of the women have already gone,' he told her, and when she opened her mouth to protest, added, 'You can't take risks, Betty, in your condition.'

It was the first time they had referred to her 'condition'. Betty shrank from the word, and recovered only to say, 'And you? What about you taking risks? Aren't you the father?'

They stared at each other in bewilderment, each wanting to make something of this moment, something memorable. Instead, neither could make the gesture: it was not the moment for one so private.

The pace of life, once a steady jog through the familiar routine, underwent a change, now seeming to race as if to a finish. Only no one thought about the finish because it was unthinkable. Something had been exposed – the stupidity of their presence here – and it was like a new rift, open and raw, that had been suddenly revealed at their feet.

Yet when the attack came, no one was in the least prepared. Horses galloped over the cobblestones in the night, there was a wild banging at the doors but if anyone dared open their shutters a crack to look out, only shadowy figures wrapped in blankets were to be seen and no one could tell if these were their own *mineros*, in rebel dress, or strangers from outside. Lighting flares, they moved on up the hill to the mine. Once there, the flares merged and multiplied, fire springing up and spreading like a lighted screen.

The men, pulling on their boots, ran up the hill too, cursing at the shortage of firearms among them. Women were ordered to remain indoors and open the doors to no one before daylight.

By dawn, the rebels had left. The works on the hill were smoking. The men were attempting to put out the fire. They returned later, black with soot and ash. Davey, one of them, sat down to pull off his boots while Betty and Lupe boiled water in cans for his bath, then began to laugh although he so rarely did. Betty, scandalised, standing by with towels, asked how he could think to laugh. Davey reported how they had passed Tough Tansy's house on their way up in the dark and seen her seated on the porch in her pink flannel nightgown, a gun across her knees, defying the rebels to approach. 'And Fred?' 'We found him this morning, under the bed,' Davey told her, then stopped laughing to add, 'They got the wrong house: they thought it was the overseer's.'

Later in the day they discovered that all the rebels had not left so quickly; one band had gone down into the town where they did find the overseer and trussed him up and demanded a 'loan' of cash which he had been compelled to let them have; after cutting the telegraph wires, they had released him but also sacked the police station and broken open the gaol, freeing all the prisoners. They had been rounding up all the mules and the arms they could lay their hands on when the cry of '*¡Los federales!*' had gone out and it was as if a whirlwind swept them along in a storm of dust.

The villagers went down to drag away the dead and bury them before the heat and the turkey buzzards made the task too foul. They discovered that not all the rebels had escaped; the federals were lining up some stragglers they had caught against the wall of the Casa de la Moneda and were shooting them one by one.

Lupe's brother had watched, and when he returned that night, told them how he had seen one rebel bend to remove his shoes and hand them to another before going to be executed. 'He was *valiente*, valiant,' he said, his eyes shining with admiration and awe.

The management of the mines had gone into a huddle and tried to find a way of sending a message to the headquarters to apprise them of their losses and the need to arm and protect themselves against future attacks.

Instead, word came that the women were to pack essentials and prepare to be evacuated as soon as transport had been arranged for them. They were to be taken down to the Company's hacienda below to wait. Once a train could be commandeered and an escort of guards provided, they would be taken to San Luis Potosí and from there to Mexico City.

'And the men?' Betty asked. 'You?' She held on to a chair and stared at Davey. 'Betty,' he replied, 'it's only till things settle down again. They will,' he assured her, but she seemed stricken and would not move. It was Lupe who ran around, gathering up the small garments they had been preparing for the child, and packing them in baskets, then knelt to take the slippers off Betty's feet and push on her walking shoes. Betty had never let her do that before.

The families had been ordered to gather at Mrs Moran's since she alone had living space large enough for the Cornish community. It was not large enough for comfort though and no one slept except for some of the small children who lay across laps or on shoulders, unconscious of the pandemonium around them. The men stood at the windows with whatever arms they could muster, in heroic attitudes they themselves found somewhat ridiculous, while some of the women tried to be helpful to Mrs Moran, beside herself with anxiety, crying, 'And I'd just put a batch of bread to rise, it's baking day tomorrow. Oh, will it all go to waste?'

Davey lost sight of Betty in the crowd that resembled an anthill someone had stoned, ants running crazily in all directions, but when the wagons the manager had obtained drew up at the door under cover of darkness that evening, he went in search of her to make sure she got on one. He found that she was lying in Mrs Moran's bed upstairs, surrounded by panic-stricken women. She was paler than Davey had ever seen her, biting her lips and drenched with perspiration. When he touched her hand, she did not seem to see him, her eyes were glazed with pain, her yellow hair tangled about her head.

'Her time's come,' Mrs Moran informed him. The emergency had brought her to her senses; she spoke quietly.

'It can't. It's too early.'

'Early it is.'

As they tried to bring Betty some relief by wiping her face with a wet towel and giving her water to drink in sips, the crowd in the room below began to pile into the wagons; the drivers were urging them to hurry.

'I can't,' Betty wept, 'I can't go, Davey.'

'You must. We must,' he told her as gently as possible. With Mrs Moran's help, he rolled her in blankets and carried her out to the last wagon to leave the village. They made room for her on a bench as best they could but there was no comfort to be found for Betty. She cried out for a doctor, her sisters, her father, and it was a sad thing that they could bring her no one. Once the wagons began to lurch their way downhill over the cobblestones, her pain grew intense. She clutched at Davey's hands, digging her nails into them so that she drew blood. She was bleeding herself, copiously. 'Slowly, slowly,' Davey begged the driver but the cartwheels trundled over the stones heedlessly.

Chapter 8

Sad it is to live in the midst of revolutions.
James Skewes in A.C. Todd, *The Search for Silver*, 1977

The party of Cornish families that left that day often told the tale of their journey – how they were taken down the hill in darkness to the hacienda below where none had ever set foot before and found that what had been spoken of in tones of awe was now little more than a blackened shell. It had been occupied by alternating troops of rebels and federals; both had participated in its destruction: the courtyard had been used as a stable for their horses and mules, and the men had slept on soiled bedding or straw, their firearms and boots under them so they would not be stolen by their comrades, while the *soldaderas* lit fires with the furniture to cook them their stews and make them their tortillas. There had evidently been drunken brawls, shattered glass lay everywhere and had to be swept up so the refugees could spread out their blankets for the night. Fires were made of twigs and brush so they could brew tea and as they sat or slept on stone floors thick with animal droppings and dirt, they felt themselves for the first time no different from the Mexicans they had lived among.

Into this encampment, Betty's almost lifeless body was carried, causing a hush to fall upon the pandemonium. Some of the women hurried their children away so they would not see or hear, others tried to erect a screen around her of blankets and shawls so she would not be seen at all in her distressing state, and to draw Davey away from her side. Some tried to help and, by the ashen light of dawn, finally delivered Betty of her child, in the course of which they lost her, saving only the infant.

Everything appeared to happen at one time: the vehicle to take them to the nearest railhead arrived and so did the minister, Edgar Butler. Too late to minister to Betty, he led Davey away while the women washed and prepared Betty for burial, then tried to persuade him to proceed with the party and the infant, but Davey would not relinquish what he saw as his last duty to Betty and insisted on preparing a coffin for her out of crates that some of the families gave for the purpose.

Together with the minister he returned to the abandoned miners' village and from there uphill in the cart to the stony graveyard. The sound of its wheels on the cobblestones ground with an iron sound that seemed to lament the harshness of Betty's fate. They met with no one on the way but, on looking back over his shoulder at the empty cottages, Davey did see a small figure slipping along the side of the street after them as unobtrusively as possible. It was Lupe who had come out to see who went by in the cart and followed it as though she sensed what it contained. Davey halted, beckoned to her and helped her in. So it was the three of them together that dug the grave outside the walled precinct of the cemetery with the pickaxes and shovels they had brought along. By dusk it was ready and they buried her before dark, piling rocks upon the grave to guard it from coyotes.

After leaving Lupe in the village with her family – she threw herself at her mother and they saw her being drawn into the woman's shawl for comfort – Davey seemed not to know what to do or where to go next and stood staring at the empty street as if waiting for it to fill with people again. The minister took him by the elbow, reminding him he now had a child to take care of, and escorted him down to the Hacienda de la Soledad. They found the Cornish party had left except for Mrs Moran and the infant who waited for his return, and that they had been joined by a circus troupe in search of shelter, all huddling around a fire made of whatever furniture remained and draped in curtains for warmth. They had abandoned their elephant, their lions and their bears but el Gran Hernandez the Great had brought his monkeys with him, dressed in their little frilled frocks and waistcoats stitched with little bells that still rang. And, more than fortunately for Betty's child, la Bella Isadora had given birth a short while ago herself, to a stillborn baby, and on seeing the tiny infant wrapped and mewling in Mrs Moran's shawl, took it to her own full breast, pressing a brown nipple to its blindly searching mouth. When the unnamed child first opened his eyes, it would have been the two painted eyebrows above her dark eyes and the head of black ringlets caught up in a bright ribbon that he would have seen, and her breast in its bed of yellow satin and lace that he would have reached for. Davey was brought to a

144

halt by the sight, and the minister and Mrs Moran had to come to his side to assist him to a seat and assure him it was for the best. Then, keeping in mind their situation and the urgent need to join the rest of the party, they collected their belongings and climbed into the cart that took them all to the railway station.

Here they found that British or American passports were required for each traveller; the '*cirqueros*' had neither but when the officer in charge saw the English child being suckled by one of them, he dropped his eyes and silently allowed them on to the vehicle. Hernandez even managed to keep one monkey on each shoulder, clutching at his ears for security and hovering anxiously around Isadora and the babe as if they too would have liked to climb into her lap for sustenance.

At the railway station they caught up with the other Cornish families who could not believe their eyes when they saw Betty's child at the swarthy *cirquera*'s breast. Women held their handkerchiefs to their mouths in shock, men found no words to speak to the bereaved father. But once seated in their carriages, flying British and American flags prominently, they found the novelty of it all soon dwindled beside the terrors they were certain faced them as they made their way across the plain under threat of raids by the rebels.

For fear of finding the tracks blown up, the driver took the engine at an excruciatingly slow crawl and, at one point, when the coal gave out, it shuddered to a halt. The men swarmed out into the canyon, searching for brush-wood as a substitute. Steam hissed from the exhausted engine, and the families, now quite silent, waited for raiders to appear from behind the ridges or out of the arroyos. When the men returned with wood and the engine was fuelled, they moved on, but that very night they were halted by raiders waiting behind a hill. Shots rang out and when they came to a standstill, figures out of their nightmares entered the carriages. They were strung with bandoliers and dressed in cotton pyjamas and khaki coats; most were barefoot, or in rope sandals, giving away their peasant origins. Some had a picture of the Virgin of Guadalupe in their straw hats. They walked calmly through the carriages, politely asking for 'loans' to pay for the army of the Revolution. When they came across la Bella Isadora and her fair babe, they smiled and passed on but stopped to shake hands with Hernandez the Great's two tiny monkeys who seemed both awed and flattered, clutching at their fingers and baring their teeth in little, frightened grins. The men and women in their seats were searching their pockets and bags for coins and watches when they heard the whistle of a train approaching at speed. It was a troop train and the raiders leapt out, springing on to their horses – some horses of blood, some nags, most without stirrups or saddles – and went streaming up the gaunt hillside from which an avalanche of pebbles and gravel poured down, deafeningly. The miners' families, seeing that the federals had arrived, leaned out of their windows, waving hats and scarves and calling 'Hurrah!'

But the engine driver had run away and hidden and they had to wait while the troops fanned out to search for him, so they allowed themselves a break in which to step out of the suffocating carriages and boil tea in a billy and eat the bread they had brought with them, meagre and gritty with sand as it was. Davey was handed some but seemed not to know what to do with it, staring at it uncomprehendingly. Around him was nothing but the sun-seared plain and its invisible cracks and rents. Night fell and, in that uninterrupted darkness, the stars surged downwards till they seemed close enough to touch, and burn. Silenced, they all waited, only the whimpering of the newborn and the wailing of coyotes to voice their fears for them.

At daybreak a new team of engine driver and fireman arrived and, with a roar of the smokestack and the shriek of a whistle, they were able to move on, smoke and cinders flying backwards into the carriages.

Tiqui-taca, rucu-raca . . . through the plains of flat brushwood and grey rubble, unbroken except for a lonely hut of adobe in a desiccated cornfield or a corral of thorn trees where a few beasts stood with their heads hanging low. And once they passed, without stopping, a railway station that was more like a stage setting or a mirage than anything real so that they could never later vouch wholeheartedly for the authenticity of what they remembered seeing there. In a totally sere and empty landscape, a train was already standing, its carriages and engine battle-weary in the dust, armed men in sandals and sombreros sprawled on the roofs of the carriages, but seated on a flat car, painted a startling red and embellished with gilt, was their captain upon a barber's chair, resplendent under a sombrero the size of a cartwheel, and his feet extended towards two bootblacks, one for each boot, polishing the cracked and filthy leather with enthusiasm. In his left hand he held a bottle of beer and the right clasped the waist of a woman in a bridal gown and a Spanish shawl. They were ringed by a band of musicians fiddling away madly what some recognised as '*Adelita*', known to be Pancho Villa's favourite song.

As their own train passed slowly, cautiously by, they asked each other if that had been Pancho Villa himself – Pancho Villa who was said to wage war by rail, moving his men, his stores, even a field hospital and a gallows for traitors, along the tracks laid by President Porfirio Díaz, now fled – and if this was a presentiment of the new Mexico, the one they would not stay to see. To Davey these were all scenes out of an evil dream that he had to endure without knowing if he would wake from it and life be restored to normality again.

In this manner, they arrived eventually at San Luis Potosí, and here Davey roused himself to send a telegram to the Hammer family in Mexico City. They had heard nothing from Betty for so long and now they received the news. They had heard of the troubles in the mining country and feared for Betty's safety but had not been prepared for calamity of this order. When Davey arrived with the child, they were shaken but determined to help in whatever way they could. They had not expected Mrs Moran, however, still less the *cirqueros*; the latter created a great stir in the household. The nursing mother was led to the kitchen for refreshment, while Mrs Moran took tea in the parlour with Mrs Hammer and described the journey.

When la Bella Isadora left later on, she made a request – 'Name the child Pablo,' she said, 'for the child I had' – while Mrs Moran was escorted to a boarding house in the city that was run by a friend of hers. As for the baby, he was taken into the Hammers' nursery in the care of their nursemaid. The Hammers assured Davey they would take the infant with them, the situation in Mexico having finally persuaded them it was time to close up home and business here and return to Cornwall, where they would convey him safely to Betty's family.

After making preparations to return to the mines, Davey went in to look at his son asleep in a cradle full of flannel and lace and found himself in such a tangle of emotions, all of which had as much to do with Betty as with their son and which he found impossible to articulate or to convey, that he left the house and went out on to the street without a word, certain he would never be able to speak of this to anyone.

Betty's father did not survive her for long and it was Gertie and Sarah who took charge, now committed to remaining unmarried and raising the child. The air of self-sacrifice and duty was as palpable in their house as the bleakness of the surrounding quarries, the nearby red-brick chapel and the need to economise on food and coal fires in a household with no income but what the child's father was able to send them. It was what the child would grow up in, an austerity like a chill in the blood. He suffered continually from colds and chilblains. 'The poor mite', everyone called him.

Davey himself returned to the mines although they were almost completely abandoned, the miners' village more or less deserted; he had need of employment after all. But the Revolution was by no means over: there were no supplies to be had and no way of transporting the ore to the smelters or the product to the mint. The trains did not run according to any schedule; there would be a ringing silence, then the shriek of a whistle and rattle of wheels along the tracks when they were least expected, and a train might appear on the plain below but whether it was the federals who were protecting it with their arms or rebels who had commandered it, no one could tell. When horses were heard riding into a village, everyone went into hiding, doors were locked and windows shut till it was safe to emerge and see what had been looted, what remained, who was still alive and who dead, swinging by the neck from a telegraph pole in a net of flies.

At the mines, shafts were allowed to fall in and water to accumulate and rise. The machinery was gradually looted and pilfered and sold for scrap in the markets of Guanajuato and Mexico City. Davey and the few other men who remained spent their nights in playing cards and drinking (Davey who had never touched a drop now drank heavily), their days in sleeping for lack of any work to be done.

Some of them began to wonder if the time had not come to return home so it was almost a stroke of good fortune when war broke out in Europe, giving them an active reason to do so. The news had been slow to reach them – it was brought back from San Luis Potosí by the man who had gone in an attempt to collect their wages, unpaid for months. Davey, together with the others, left immediately to book a passage to England and, on arriving in Liverpool, found the country caught up in a wild wave of patriotism. Men were volunteering in masses, and he joined them. After receiving basic training in a camp in Norfolk, he was sent with a division of Rawlinson's Fourth Army to France. To die there would have been a release but he was only wounded, in the Battle of the Somme, and shipped back to England to recover.

Madge Richards, who also found the war a relief from

the tedium of her life, nursed him in the hospital set up in the manorial hall of her village in Gloucestershire. He shocked the young woman by begging her to bring him some brandy to ease the pain in his leg; the daughter of a clergyman, she had never touched spirits in her life and would not have for anyone less handsome and romantic than this widower from Mexico. When he was released, she set herself to reform him. She did this by marrying him, which soon returned Davey to sobriety.

On setting up house in a pebble-dashed cottage by the sea where Davey found work at a fishmonger's in the village, they fetched Paul to live with them. Betty's sisters had worn themselves out with their care of him through his infancy but saw him leave with reluctance; they agreed that his place was with his father, of course, but privately confessed their doubts as to Madge's fitness for the role of stepmother. 'She's not had to do with children ever,' they sighed, 'the poor little mite.' As for Paul, he felt he had entered a house of strangers; he could form no relationship with his father, a man who suffered from having once known the wildness and space of mining country in the West and who, now become no more than a shop-hand in a seaside village, said little, and frequently, even in the wettest weather, went for long walks along the cliffs under lowering clouds and spitting rain, refusing any company. As for Paul's stepmother, she washed and she cleaned and she polished as if their lives depended on it, and watched out for any alcohol that Davey might resort to or bring into the house. She could not see Paul or his father as anything but agents of possible weakness and trouble.

It was clear to Paul that, as soon as he left school, it would be best for him to look for work elsewhere. He found a position in Liverpool as a shipping clerk, lodged in a boarding house near the docks with several other clerks, and spent his Sundays walking by the estuary and watching the tugs draw the ships in to port followed by flocks of clamouring seagulls. They planted in him the idea of flight, of escape, while the looming warehouses and the shipping and insurance firms of the city closed in and blocked him.

When war was declared in 1939, it might have provided him with a way out but when he went to volunteer, he was rejected on account of a formerly undetected – and certainly non-threatening – curvature of the spine. He took the rejection hard and was not consoled by the job he was given instead as a storekeeper of army supplies, seeing them loaded on to ships and sent off to the far-flung battlefields where he would have preferred to be himself. Once the war was over, he returned to his old job at the shipping firm but this was hardly satisfying any more. Then he found he was able to get a cheap passage on one of their boats to America. It would have been fitting if the boat had sailed for Mexico but instead it sailed northwards to Canada. When it halted to refuel in Portland, Maine, Paul found they would be held up longer for repairs and disembarked to travel for what he thought would be a few days, up the coast of Maine.

In a fishing village where he stopped to eat a bowl of clam chowder, he saw a notice glued to the window, advertising a vacancy in a local fishing business. He had never acted on an impulse before but now he did and went around to meet the owners. At the end of the interview, a brief and brisk one, they took him home to eat with the family and among four brothers he found one sister, Madeleine, the youngest who, never before having met anyone from outside their village, appeared as fascinated by him as perhaps Betty had been on meeting a miner visiting from Mexico. As for Paul, he found himself engulfed by family in a way he had not ever experienced. After informing the captain in Portland that he would not be rejoining the passengers, he stayed on to work for the family. On his frequent visits to their home, Madeleine would contrive always to sit beside him. The family, noting her infatuation, stirred in discomfort: they liked him well enough but she was the baby, many years too young for this silent stranger. Besides, he was not of their faith, however irreproachable his bookkeeping might be. Each brother tried to dissuade her from her ardour, leaving her tearful but determined. What proved harder for her to alter was Paul's own hesitation at accepting this adoration from someone he saw as practically a child. It was Madeleine's mother who, seeing their suffering and restraint, finally gave her the encouragement she craved. 'He is not one of us,' she said, 'and you can never be married in church, but it seems he is the one for you.' Of Paul, she asked that he remain in their home and village so that they would not have to part with their daughter.

They married and Paul found his married existence a complete escape from the loneliness he had known till then but was also often overcome by the sheer numbers and noise and apt to fall silent and feel lost among them. At such moments, Madeleine would emerge from the crowd and find a reason for him to return to the small room where he kept the books and where he could disappear for a little respite. She would pat his shoulder in sympathy and he would clasp her hand gratefully, but without a word.

It was many years before they had a child – as if they had been intimidated and discouraged by the large numbers all around them, the brothers being married and with numerous progeny housed in cottages they had built in the family yard by the sea – and when Eric was born, Madeleine proved as protective of him as of the stranger she had married. They both personified for her the outside world that she herself had never stepped into – except on the one visit back to Cornwall that she and Paul undertook when they left Eric with his grandfather in the pebble-dashed cottage by the sea where he played with a toy train filled with sparkling flakes of ore till his step-grandmother, entering the room with a teapot under a cosy, said, 'Now don't go filling his head with all that nonsense.'

It was the only time Davey Rowse was known to have spoken to anyone of the mines in Mexico where he had once worked, and it was in his grandson Eric's head that he buried a flake of golden nonsense that he had once found in Mexico's mountains.

PART IV

La Noche de los Muertos

In the creation story of the Huichol Indians, when gods and goddesses first appeared on earth, it was in darkness. They set out to find light, led by the fire god, Tatéwari. When they arrived at the sea, they witnessed the sun rising from a tunnel in the mountains and it cast its light upon the earth for the first time.

The last of the gods to arrive there was Kauyumari, the deer spirit. In the newborn light, the others could see that it had left round, green, rosette-like tracks across the desert.

Tatéwari the fire god bade them to collect these green spoors and eat them for they were sacred food, the peyote that grows on the holy mountain, Wirikúta.

First they made offerings and sang and danced in thanksgiving. Then Tatéwari the shaman fed each one some of the sacred food, and they found they were able to hear the songs that Tatéwari and Kauyumari had been singing about the pilgrimage they had come on.

They understood that Kauyumari had left these tracks so others could follow and also experience the time of their ancestors and understand where they came from and who they were.

That is why the peyote is never completely uprooted; the tap root is left in the soil so more peyote may grow and show the way.

Chapter 9

Coming out of the Cathedral, he had to steady himself at the top of the stairs before he could descend them: the afternoon light had struck him such a blow and blinded him too. The plaza was quiet at this hour, the white dust disturbed only by the wind that lifted and dispersed it. All around the great houses of the rich stood, shut-faced and grim because now they were not great and not rich. Only the height of the stone walls and the width of the doorways made them seem so but the carved oak doors were gone and so were the shutters, their place taken by iron bars or wooden planks. Windows gaped and doors opened on to darkness now. Built to cast all other buildings into eclipse, they were themselves eclipsed and the museum that supposedly recorded these vicissitudes was shut too – for the afternoon, or the holiday, or both.

There was no food to be had here and Eric felt in need of some as did the thin, silent dog that had waited for him at the door and now followed him again with hopeful loyalty, to the nearby smaller plaza. Here there were trees, a bandstand of filigree ironwork and stalls where tortillas were being patted out on hot griddles and meat stirred into rich *mole* sauces in great earthenware pots. Eric slid on to a bench at one stall and had an enamel plate passed down the long table to him along with an assortment of dishes to which he helped himself, while the dog crawled under the table, out of sight, hoping to avoid confrontation with larger, sturdier brutes prowling around for bones.

People had come in from surrounding villages for the festival, and at the stalls around the plaza were buying themselves straw hats and baskets, kitchenware and shoes. A photographer had set up a booth and was posing families against a canvas backdrop painted with scenes of flowering gardens, moonlit lakes and palatial mansions. Sometimes they adorned themselves with the striped serapes and the velvet sombreros trimmed with silver that he lent them and sometimes they strapped on bandoliers, held wooden guns and mounted wooden horses, but some posed simply as themselves, barefooted and bareheaded in the midst of all the painted splendour.

He was doing much more brisk business, Eric could see, than the painter of *retablos* in his wooden shack; only a few customers stopped to tell him their tales of miraculous recoveries from snakebite, fire, smallpox and accidents or escapes from stampeding horses and runaway buses, which he painted for them on small tablets of tin and wood that they could take to the cathedral as offerings.

Eric strolled across to watch for a while and wished he

too had a dramatic tale to tell that the painter could record for him. Lacking one, he considered the undramatic scenes from his life he might have enjoyed seeing the man paint: the kitchen in Boston, Em and himself at the table under a yellow lamp, the cat Shakespeare seated beside them with his white paws tucked into his black fur; or his father and himself picking their way around the rock pools of the Maine coast with their heads lowered to the salt sea spray; or himself as a child, kneeling before a fireplace in Cornwall . . . But you couldn't hold together these disparate scenes, or meld them into a coherent whole. He mentally added a Mexican background, ochre and dun with a mountainscape in dramatic purples and crimsons. The painter would certainly be able to provide that, in confident brush strokes, and yet – something would still be lacking. Eric could not place his finger on it but could clearly see a gap in one corner, like a smudge or a blur. He moved away, as if in search of what might fill it.

He considered giving some custom to the old potter whose simple earthenware pots seemed to be doing less brisk business than another vendor's tin and plastic kitchenware. Em would surely appreciate something handmade, possibly one of the coffee-coloured coffee mugs decorated with a wonderfully free swirl of paint; he could see it placed companionably by her elbow on her desk as she worked and suddenly felt that he could hardly bear to wait to resume that life, to bask in her calm, assured company again and not be solitary and adrift any more. The coffee mug acquired a talismanic quality before his eyes. It would be difficult to carry such an object safely back to Boston but, after a brief hesitation, he decided to take the risk and had the old man wrap one up in a sheet of newspaper for him. Then the price he asked, so low, so humble, shamed him and he wished he could have purchased more but, carefully putting away the package in his backpack, he moved on, knowing that now he must buy something to take to the cemetery, an offering to his ancestors: that was why he was here. What should it be and where would he find it?

Round and round the plaza he wandered, the same people looking up to see him pass again and again, wondering at his purpose – and purposelessness. Of course he had to make an offering – '*¡Claro!*' he heard a chorus of voices ring out in his head as if he had gathered a crowd of spectators around him, and their voices rose in a crescendo, so he reached out for a spray of white chrysanthemums and heard a deep sigh of satisfaction at his purchase, his dutiful observation of the rituals, and felt their relief enter into him.

As he handed over the pesos in payment and carried away the bouquet, the church bells rang out to announce the hour, three o'clock, and at that instant rockets shot into the sky, long whining shrieks followed by explosions that echoed back and forth between the hills. In the brilliant light of day, they could not be seen, only heard, and heard they were: they were the announcement for *los muertitos* to return home and for the living to go to the cemetery to receive them by washing, cleaning and decorating their tombs, lighting candles to show them the way, and welcoming them with flowers.

He joined the procession of people, family groups mostly, out of the plaza and on to the dirt road that wound uphill past houses of adobe and tile that were clearly abandoned and in ruins, doors hanging from their hinges, barred windows opening on to scenes of fallen walls, painted plaster turned to flakes of dust, cacti and convolvuli growing where floors had been. Perhaps these were the houses where the Cornish miners had once lived? Turkey buzzards hovered over them in the livid air, with their wings outstretched and their wingtips lifted to catch the currents that bore them up, then swirled them slowly around. On the rocks, lizards – gaunt, withered – skittered away at the sound of footsteps on the stones and disappeared into cracks or whipped around the baking stones. Grasshoppers shot out of the way like seeds exploding and scattering.

A man and his wife sat in the sparse shade of a mesquite tree eating the tortillas they had brought with them; their burro, tethered to the tree, seemed asleep on its legs except for the ears that remained alert and twitched away flies.

Someone had put up a stall of reeds and planks and was selling bottled drinks, orange and red and green, for the thirsty.

They shuffled on through the dust, passing the stone walls and entrance to the *palenque* that Eric had been told was where bets of many thousand pesos had once been won and lost, not to speak of ranches and mines, but that was now closed. Yet he could have sworn it was full of people, for he heard voices rising in a state of hysteria as spectators betted on and cheered the brilliant, spurred roosters. Even the dog at his heels lifted its small stumps of ears as if at the noise. Dust flew and Eric could sense the great crowd packed into a small space even if he saw no one.

Of the mine there was no trace. Perhaps the cave gouged into the hillside had once been an entrance to it, and perhaps the tumbled remnants of a stone wall around a bare and thorny space had once been a *hacienda de beneficio*, but the shafts had fallen in, back into the rubble, or else had been blown down and dispersed by the wind.

The cemetery lay on the flank of the hill, below the summit. The entrance of two pillars of stone set in the low whitewashed wall of adobe was hung with banners of white and yellow paper perforated with the figures of dancing skeletons that rustled and rattled with macabre life in the wind that blew here unimpeded. People were passing through it, carrying sheaves of flowers, baskets of food and drink, bundles of candles and pots of copal, blankets and children. In the cemetery they dispersed, each in the direction of the graves they had come to tend.

Eric, not knowing where to go, stayed by the entrance where a single cypress tree grew, so long and spindly that it looked like a pole thrust into the ground; it cast practically no shadow. No one paid him the least attention: he might have been another pole, or cypress, planted there.

People were slipping silently up the path in all directions, their feet shuffling through the grey suede of the dust. The families that had already arrived were at work washing and scrubbing what tombstones there were, straightening the crosses that were listing to one side, filling rusty cans with water from a tap for the fresh flowers they had brought, lighting copal and candles whose flames bent and wavered and twisted grotesquely in the wind.

Eric became awkwardly aware that he alone was doing

nothing, just standing there with a sheaf of flowers in his hands. He had no idea where to place them. Somehow he had assumed his grandmother was buried here and that he would recognise her grave when he came upon it, that it would have her name carved upon it, as neglected as it might be, and he would offer her his flowers. Now it occurred to him it would not be so: she could not be buried here, in a Catholic cemetery in the the shadow of their chapel which stood on the rock above.

The truth was that he had no idea where she might be buried. He had merely assumed it would be here where she died. (Em's face with a familiar expression of worried solicitude flitted past him like one of the pale moths blundering through the dusk.)

He detached himself from the trunk of the cypress tree that was now casting a shadow across the white hillside, more like the shadow cast by a sundial than by a tree, and began to stumble up the path in the direction of the chapel where he might meet a priest he could ask where the foreigners were buried who had once lived here and worked in the mines.

As the dusk thickened with the addition of the smoke of copal, candles shone everywhere in the walled enclosure of the cemetery, hundreds of them, bending and righting themselves and then bending again, now illuminating the groups gathered around the graves, now casting them into shadow.

As he drew his jacket close about him, someone seated by the path extended a bottle to him. 'Have a drink,' he invited in slurred tones, and Eric, taking the bottle and suppressing a quaver of squeamishness, drank. 'It seems you needed it,' the man said, watching. And it was strange but Eric, who understood so little Spanish and no Indian tongue, understood every word spoken to him, and it seemed that he too was understood when he spoke, with no trouble at all, just as though he were in a trance.

'I did,' Eric agreed, handing back the bottle.

'You have come from far? You look like those men who used to run the mines here, the Cousin Jacks as they called them in my father's and grandfather's day.'

'They worked in the mines? So did mine – my grandfather.'

'But yours left. Ours stayed, and died.'

Eric looked to the side of the man to see if there was a gravestone with a name on it but there was none, just a mound of earth and a cross stuck into it on which initials and dates were carved roughly with a knife. Pickle jars filled with flowers, the spokes of red gladioli and sunbursts of yellow chrysanthemums, perched on the mound. A woman and a boy were lighting candles and planting them in the earth.

'I know one who did stay, and died,' Eric said.

'Here?'

'I think so. I believe so,' Eric said, then thanked him for the drink and moved on. He was both surprised and shamed by the ease with which the words came to his mouth, how readily he had imparted so private a matter to a stranger.

But then, there was this curious sensation of not being among strangers at all.

At another group he lingered to breathe in the aroma of warm, baked food. The woman who was engaged in feeding her children as well as the dead, seeing his look, held out her basket and asked if he would like a *pasta*, it was what she had brought in case her children turned hungry.

'A *pasta*?' Eric asked, accepting a warm pastie that fitted into his palm like a soft little dove. He bit into it and as his teeth met with the meat and potatoes inside the crust, he thought he had never eaten anything so good. He did not think she would expect payment from him here in the cemetery so he only thanked her but she had already turned aside and was bringing out more pots and dishes from her basket, her children crawling closer to this source of nourishment.

There were not large family gatherings around every grave; some had only one person alone come to clear the place of a year's worth of weeds, discard the offerings of the year before and fill a rusted tin can with fresh flowers. Some graves had no one at all attending them, and other visitors to the cemetery, out of pity, left a few marigolds or a stalk of amaranth so the dead would not feel forgotten or excluded. By including them, their families seemed to be filling in whatever empty spaces there might be.

Under a dust-coloured, skeletal mesquite tree, a man leaned, his arms folded, and from under the brim of his hat he stared sorrowfully at a grave a small distance away. Eric stopped to keep him company although he did not appear to want any. The man did eventually notice him, however, for he sighed and said, 'So there she lies, alone, and she was always, always afraid of that.'

'Your wife?' Eric found himself asking.

'My Ana,' the man said as if no other label were needed. 'Her father gave her to me when she was fifteen years old and said, "Take care of her." See, that is how I took care

165

– left her alone here –' and he shuddered with a great, dramatic sigh.

Eric looked away but could not resist asking, 'Was it an illness? Or an accident?'

'She gave birth,' the man said. 'Her last act.'

'And the child?' Eric murmured, scarcely parting his lips. He would not ordinarily have dared question a stranger so but there was a sense here, on this hillside, in the dark and with the fumes of copal blowing like mist over it, that they were not strangers but kith, communicating in a language they would not ordinarily use. It belonged to this night, a country in itself. 'And the child?' he repeated.

'The child,' the man turned to him with a smile, 'she is an *angelita* in Heaven and will never know the grief of life.'

That thought seemed to lighten the man's sorrow, at least momentarily, and he detached himself from the tree trunk and approached the grave. Eric said after him, 'My father – was born – and lived –' but the man did not seem to hear.

Someone on the hillside was playing a guitar; the notes fell one after the other, like drops, or days. A voice was singing a mournful ballad although not mournfully.

Eric, moving towards the sound, saw a group of men seated on the rocks and gravel, passing around a bottle of tequila as they listened, sometimes joining in the refrain. One of them, seeing Eric, turned around to tell him, 'It's for that old rascal, Perseverancio from the La Malinche mine. Good for nothing, worked just enough to earn a bottle of tequila and drink it, but he liked to sing, he did,' and he laughed to think of the good times. 'Quite a voice he had, that *borracho*, he did.'

'Ah, not anything like mine,' the guitarist broke off to contradict, then launched into another song.

Perhaps later they would be too drunk even to walk down the hill but at the moment they seemed to be a wonderfully contented band of men sitting on the ground with their bottle of tequila and their memories of other times, drinking. When they opened a fresh bottle, one of them sprinkled some from it in a sign of the cross over the grave so the dead Perseverancio might have his share.

Eric, beginning to feel the chill of the darkened hillside, sank down on a mound of earth – at a slight distance so they would not think they had to keep passing the bottle of tequila to him – and huddled in his jacket, clutching the chrysanthemums to him; they smelt more than ever of funerals. He watched the figures that rose up and sank down like the shadows cast by candles and wondered if any of them might tell him something of his grandparents' time.

Stars began to flower in the sky, like jasmines opening in the dark, and there was surely jasmine flowering in the cemetery because he could detect its fragrance over the heavy perfume of copal burning in censers over the graves.

But perhaps it was only the perfume used by a woman, more expensively dressed than the others, who sat beside a grave with a headstone decorated with an enormous tinsel wreath that caught the flickering candlelight and glittered like a wreath of bluebottles.

She saw him staring and said, 'Big, eh? Ex-pen-seev, eh?' nodding at that gaudy ring. 'The most *costoso* I could find in the stinking little town down there.'

He was taken aback by her tone, so out of keeping with

the sepulchral atmosphere of the night and the place. Her voice, too, was raucous, lit with the flame of liquor.

'It's what he deserves, you see,' she said, and made a gesture at her own outfit, the shiny purple satin of it, the ruches, the frills and the flounces of it. 'He was a *puto* and I'm glad he is in his grave but he did leave me something, after all,' and she laughed and jangled the bracelet on her wrist.

Eric had no idea what to say – he had never met anyone like her – but she clearly wanted conversation.

'Do you live here – in this town?' he asked, clearing his throat.

'Not I,' she laughed. 'Left it the day after the funeral. I have travelled from far to do this. Otherwise, I knew, he will send his ghost, his *sombra*, to –' and she put her finger to her temple and made the clicking sound of a gun. '*Puto*,' she cursed – but almost fondly.

Eric became aware that she had a bottle with her because now she lifted it and drank. He marvelled at her, at the difference between her and the other women gathered around other graves with their domestic ways: he could not help a slight quiver of admiration.

She passed him the bottle of beer. 'Here,' she offered, wiping her mouth, and smearing lipstick across her cheek like a scar as she did so. 'This is the first and the last time I come,' she said, 'because now I leave for Tijuana. They say it is a place you can have luck. You know it?'

'I don't.'

'But you are *americano*?'

'Yes,' he acknowledged. What was he, after all? Perhaps that. If she wanted, then yes, he was.

'Hmm, I like them, the *americanos*,' she said thoughtfully, and Eric shifted uneasily, deciding to move. He made an ostentatious show of groaning as he got to his feet and dusted off the seat of his pants, then began to sidle towards the chapel looming overhead, telling her, 'It's time I went in there.'

She shrugged and, as he left her, he heard her say, in a rasping voice, 'The last time, you hear? Now I can turn my back on your cursed town, and don't expect to see me again.'

When Eric glanced covertly back, she was standing up, holding aloft the bottle with an unusual blatancy for a woman. 'So, take one good look, eh, at your *puta*, your whore. She made good!' Her voice rose and now she was scattering drops from the bottle over the grave and over herself as well. It was hard to say if she was laughing or crying, her voice was so hoarse and certainly she was very drunk.

A band of children, running among the tombstones and crosses on the hillside, themselves intoxicated with the night, stopped to watch her antics and burst out laughing. '*¡La borracha!*' they screamed. '*¡La borracha!*' This gave them away to their mothers who called to them, sharply, and they scattered like the last of the sparrows before darkness swallows them.

Around the grave at the foot of the stairs to the chapel, a group sat as if composed by a painter: at its head the matriarch wrapped in a shawl and her face lowered to the rosary she told incessantly while the candles on the gravestone, thick with trickling wax, flung their shadows over her seamed face; around her the family, obediently reverent, seated for what would be a long night. The wax ran and hissed among the pots of flowers and copal set

169

out. The Latin words of the rosary trickled and hissed along with them, keeping pace.

Slipping around and past them – uncertain, somewhat, that they were of solid flesh and blood and not just skeletons dressed up – he went up the broken stone steps, white in the darkness, to the chapel. It was empty, and though there was no source of light to be seen, somehow the frescoes painted inside the dome were clearly visible, depicting the saints in robes of blue and russet, wandering through gardens where lilies bloomed among cypresses and angels drifted through rose-tinted clouds. Where had these visions come from, Eric wondered, which artist had seen these cinquecento figures and radiant landscapes? His paintbrush had created a serene and formal Eden from another world.

Walking up the central aisle, Eric passed the scenes of the Stations of the Cross on either side and then thought that if the artist could imagine such agonies, such wounds, such suffering, then yes, of course he could also imagine the promise of Heaven that made it bearable.

Walking slowly and as soundlessly as possible, Eric tried to read the inscriptions and names on the stones under his feet. Many of them bore the same name, and it was the name of the family into which Doña Vera had married. He bent to peer at one and as he wiped the dust from it to see better, he became aware of someone seated on the other side of the front pew, sprawled as if drunk or exhausted after a long ride. He did not appear to be one of the villagers crowding the cemetery; none of them would have sat in this fashion in church, it would have been beyond them to do other than bow their heads and crouch.

Sliding into a pew on the other side of the aisle, the flowers across his knees, Eric studied him as unobtrusively as possible. His first impression, that this was a visitor from elsewhere, was borne out by a closer inspection, for the figure was dressed in expensive and finely tailored clothes including a waistcoat and a silk cravat around his neck. His legs were sprawled out and Eric saw the quality of his leather boots, polished to a high shine; how had he maintained that if he had walked up the dusty road with the others? In spite of his casual attitude, he did not seem comfortable, twitching frequently, crossing and recrossing his legs and fingering first his cravat and then his trousers; probably they were too tight.

The man must have become aware that he was being scrutinised because eventually he turned to Eric with a sigh and now Eric could see his swarthy, heavy-jowled face, the eyebrows growing like an animal's fur across his forehead, and the mouth downturned in what was unmistakably a belligerent scowl.

'So, someone has been sent up from the hacienda to bring me something after all,' he said in a voice that resembled a wagon full of orc lumbering through a tunnel to reach Eric.

'I'm sorry, I'm not – not sure what you mean,' Eric stammered.

The man raised an eyebrow and the small red eye under it gave him a hostile look. 'Have you not come from the Hacienda de la Soledad?'

'I have, but how did you know that?'

The man gave an approximation of a laugh and twisted his fingers inside his collar in that obsessive attempt to loosen it. 'What do I have to do but watch what goes on?' he said. 'Do you think she does not know that?'

'Doña Vera, you mean?' Eric asked, quite unnecessarily.

Removing his fingers from the collar, the man waved them in a gesture of contempt and derision. 'The one and only,' he said. 'Still playing the queen there, I'm sure. The Queen of the Sierra! What a farce.'

Eric held his breath, uncertain whether to agree or not and resolving to say nothing, give nothing away that might get back to that terrifying lady.

'I could tell you some things about that,' the man went on. 'The queen of exactly what, I could tell you. The bars and theatres where she made her living! They were not so pretty and I should know since that is where I found her.'

'Where –?' Eric could not stop himself from asking.

'In *Wien*!' the man exploded. '*Österreich*! I arrived there just when it was finished – *terminado*! She was happy enough to come away. She was a clever one and knew when it was time to leave. I should have been suspicious.'

Eric held still, saying nothing.

'How long could her luck have lasted? Do you think she could have survived? No, no, I saved her. But did she thank me for that – for her freedom, her escape? Not once. Tell her, please, from me, Roderigo *demands* that she thank him. Will you?'

Eric was about to tell him that he did not intend to return to the Hacienda de la Soledad but the man was not waiting for an answer. He went on loudly, demanding further, 'And ask her also if she remembers what day it is today. Has she forgotten? Has she no memory? In all these years, she has not remembered once!' Then he lowered his voice and asked, less rhetorically, almost with shame, 'Or did she send you with that – that bunch –?'

Eric clutched at the flowers. 'No, no,' he cried and was inexplicably afraid, chilled to the bone with fear – or perhaps it was just the chill of the stone chapel in which the darkness was intensifying, making it difficult to see across the aisle, let alone the frescoes or the dome. 'I brought them for –'

The man sighed heavily. 'Yes, I should have seen that. It is not her style,' and saying that, his head slumped to his shoulders as if sleep had overtaken him. His heavy breathing might have included the vibrato of a snore.

Eric decided to make an escape before he stirred and, rising to his feet, proceeded to do so as silently as he could manage on that stone floor. But he must have disturbed the man's sleep for he heard a voice booming out at his departing back. 'And those poor intoxicated *indios* she keeps – tell her, tell her, if she wants to be queen, she should have chosen better subjects!' A shout of laughter followed the derisive words, laughter that echoed back and forth, back and forth sacrilegiously in that still chamber. Eric, scandalised, stopped with his fingers to his lips to suppress it but the voice continued. 'Tell her, ask her,' it pursued him, 'when the time comes, where does she think they will bring her? It will be here, with me beside her – and around us *all* the *indios* she could wish!'

Then the figure of Don Roderigo began to expand. It became huge. It spat out malice and vengeance. It came storming along after Eric, shouting, 'And she had El Duque shot! You know that? When I was no longer there to protect him, she had my faithful El Duque destroyed! Is that the behaviour of a queen?'

The voice and the figure rose to such proportions that they took up the entire chapel and Eric found himself propelled through the door and out into the open with more haste than he would have liked anyone to observe.

Something seated in a bush below gave a croak of alarm and flapped away into the dark.

The darkness had intensified because the candles had now burnt low or even gone out. The wind was still blowing and even though there were no leaves or grasses through which it could be heard to pass, there was a rustling and a stirring all around. The praying and singing and murmuring by the graves was rising to a crescendo and the fragrance of flowers and copal and candles combined in a smothering odour.

Eric felt the need to be by himself, alone. He knew he would not find the grave he had searched for here. Coming down the steps from the chapel, he went around to the back to see if there was an enclosure for the alien, separate and isolated from the rest.

Of course, here too there was uneven ground, there were mounds of earth, crosses askew upon them – their threatening, admonishing shapes barely visible in the night – and thorns, stones, rubble.

The long night, the increasing chill, the effort of staying awake and alert, all became overwhelming, more than he could resist. It would only make sense to leave, return to the inn and the comfort of a warm bed, knowing he had made the effort, and failed.

Glancing up, however, he saw what must be the first light of dawn because now he could make out the outline of the mountain: the sky must have, so imperceptibly and secretly, paled. A cross became visible, mounted on the summit as if it, too, were a gigantic grave. The slope of the mountain was still shadowy with night but, as he walked towards the whitewashed wall that marked the periphery of the cemetery, he could make out a path winding up between rocks and cacti.

A young woman was descending it, with such ease and speed it was as though she did not notice the stones in her way, they were not impediments to her. She was preceded by a fragrance that was as fresh as the breeze that was blowing freely, not the heavy perfume of copal, tallow candles and funeral flowers but a much lighter, more natural one, of herbs like lavender, rosemary and thyme, mountain herbs that seemed unlikely to be growing in that hostile rubble and stoniness but perhaps were since their essence was clearly present.

Seeing Eric standing by the low wall that ringed the cemetery, she lifted her hand, holding a small bunch of grey leaves and pale flowers, and to his amazement, waved to him. He could not imagine why she acknowledged him or who she might be or why she was there, but his mind had ceased to pose questions, they were all obliterated by the wave of her hand and the pure scent of the flowers.

'I found them by the path,' she said lightly, conversationally, as if continuing a dialogue that they had already begun. 'All growing wild. I wonder the goats don't eat them.'

She came right up to the wall so that she was standing on one side of it, he on the other. In the opalescent light of dawn, he saw that her hair was so bright, it was like the petals of newly opened *zempasúchil* flowers all over her head.

He stammered, 'You – you're like a flower yourself.'

She gave him a look out of the corner of her eyes, not so much conquettishly as simply amused. 'And you – you're Paul, aren't you? I thought you might come.' She sat herself down on the wall, ready for his response.

'No,' he told her sadly, 'I'm not. Paul is my father. I'm Eric, his son.'

She gave no indication she had heard or understood. Stroking the silvery grey leaves of the nosegay in her hand, she said, almost shyly, 'You are just as I thought you would be. Dark, like Davey, and all the men in Davey's family. They say the Cornish aren't English at all, that they come from somewhere else. Have you heard that?'

'Yes,' Eric admitted, but anything he had ever heard or read on the subject went clear out of his mind in her presence. 'I think, I think they may have come from Spain – or somewhere.'

She was not too concerned with accuracy. 'Everyone comes from somewhere else,' she said, nodding towards the shifting, moving shapes and shadows behind the chapel, and added, 'Like Mexicans. They say they came from Asia, across the – the –'

'The Bering Straits,' Eric put in, relieved to remember something, to know that his mind was intact and had not been swallowed up by the eeriness of the night on the dark hill.

The name clearly meant little or nothing to her. She went on picking at the leaves in her hand and at the thread of her thoughts while Eric watched and listened, scarcely breathing. The thread she picked at seemed to waver and wander. 'Like us, from Cornwall. Such a long way to come.' Her eyes widened and Eric could see their grey, transparent glaze.

'Quite a journey,' he agreed, trying to encourage her to say more.

But she had come to the end of that thread. 'And ending here,' she said, tapping the wall she sat on so lightly.

'I couldn't find –' Eric began, then stopped short: it would be tactless, tasteless to mention the cemetery to her, and graves; how could he?

She, on the other hand, had no hesitation in doing so. 'Our graves?' she asked, quite blandly, and pointed to the hill she had descended. 'We're there. D'you know what they call it? Jews' Hill,' she told him with a laugh. 'It was the place where they buried everyone not of their faith.'

'Were there many?' Eric ventured, hesitantly.

'Oh,' she said, tilting her head and counting. 'Tough Tansy's little sister who came to help her with all the babies, and died of the cholera. Miss Lily and Miss Minnie's brother who died falling down a shaft, his foot missed its hold. Then, when the troubles began, many more. Mr Ashworth from La Malinche was shot, and Mr MacDuff died in the fire when they burnt down the ware-house, he was hiding in it, and lots more –' she broke off. 'That made people leave. Davey –?' she ventured, looking up at Eric as if in search of a resemblance, and reassurance.

'He returned to Cornwall, to be with Paul,' Eric tried to explain the abandonment to her. Perhaps she came here every year, on this night, in the hope of seeing him. The thought was painful.

Clearly she was still hurt. Determined, too, not to dwell on it or show it.

'And you've come back,' she said, choosing to misunderstand. 'I knew you would.'

Eric wanted to ask her what he could bring her. He thought of everything the Mexican families came equipped with to provide *los muertitos* for the afterlife – tequila for the drunkards, cards for the gamblers, guitars for the musical, sugar lambs and chicks for *los angelitos*. He suddenly felt the limpness of the flowers he was still clutching and awkwardly proferred them. 'I brought you flowers,' he mumbled shamefacedly: they did not seem at all the right ones for this young girl in her dress of pale blue tulle with its hem of pink roses – rather torn and tattered, he now noticed in the increasing pallid dawn light.

She took them but seemed to agree with him about their unsuitability, giving a small formal smile as one who is accustomed to the obtuseness of men. Putting them down on the wall beside her, she went on, 'Sometimes the Indians come, you know. They are pilgrims. They climb the mountain to pick the peyote cactus. It's very special, they say. It grows only here,' she motioned at the mountain at her back, 'so it's sacred.'

'I've heard of it – of the pilgrimage.'

'And one crazy old woman – not Indian, from elsewhere – she comes, too.'

'I know. I met her.'

Again she appeared to take no notice of this news from the present world. 'But the peyote gives her bad dreams, very bad. She doesn't come any more.'

'But she talks about it a lot, the pilgrimage.'

'Yes, and the Indians still come. They spend the night on the mountain. They collect peyote and eat it; it makes them dream.'

'I'd like to try.'

She gave him a slightly mocking look. 'Then come,'

she said, 'come,' and rising from the wall, turned and began to walk up the path which was now a grey stream pouring through the dark volcanic rubble in that early light.

Eric tried to follow. The wall stood between them. He intended to climb over and follow but, as he looked down for a foothold in order to do so, she disappeared. When he looked up to call and ask her to wait, he saw that she was gone. Although there was more light now than there had been before, he could see her nowhere on that barren hillside. She had left behind the chrysanthemums and they lay limp on the wall, devoid now of fragrance.

There was only the melancholy tinkling of bells and a movement of the speckled stones that proved to be young goats which had come to graze. A shepherd boy, appearing among them, gave a long sharp whistle that made them skip and skitter on their little hooves.

Below, in the town, the church bells began to ring. They rang and rang insistently, calling the dead back to their graves. The light grew brighter, the sun appeared and everyone went streaming back to where they had come from.

Acknowledgements

The author is grateful for travel grants from the Massachusetts Institute of Technology, and for hospitality from two writers' retreats in Italy, the Santa Maddalena Foundation in Donnini (Firenze) and the Centro Studi Ligure in Bogliasco (Genova).

Thanks are also due to the following publications for epigraph quotations.

Page vi: Charles Macomb Flandreu, *Viva Mexico!*, D. Appleton & Co., 1908 and 1937. University of Illinois Press, Urbana, © 1964 by the Board of Trustees, University of Illinois.

Page 3: Elizabeth Bishop, 'Arrival at Santos' (1952), from *The Complete Poems* (1927–1979), Chatto & Windus, London, and Farrar, Straus & Giroux, New York, 1983.

Page 22: Interview with André Breton by Rafael Heliodoro Valle in *Universidad*, no. 29, June 1938. Reprinted in *Mexico en el Arte*, 1986, and in a foreword by Susan Kismaric to a catalogue of Manuel Alvarez's photographs in the Museum of Modern Art, New York, 1997.

Page 59: Bernal Díaz, *The Conquest of New Spain*, 1519, 1568, translated and introduced by J. M. Cohen, Penguin, Harmondsworth, 1963.

Pages 40, 61, 128: Carl Sartorius, *Mexico and the Mexicans*, Darmstadt, London, New York, 1859, and F. A. Brockhaus Komm., Stuttgart, 1961.

Pages 98, 113: Bernal Díaz, *The Conquest of New Spain*.